# The Recipe Cops

# Titles by Keith Weaver

An Uncompromising Place
The Recipe Cops

# The Recipe Cops

Keith Weaver

Published by Iguana Books
720 Bathurst Street, Suite 303
Toronto, Ontario, Canada
M5V 2R4



Publisher: Kathryn Willms
Editor: Holly Warren
Front cover image: Courtesy of unsplash.com (Lou Levit)
Front cover design: Victoria Feistner

Library and Archives Canada Cataloguing in Publication
Weaver, Keith, 1947-, author
The recipe cops / Keith Weaver.

Issued in print and electronic formats.

ISBN 978-1-77180-185-0 (paperback).--ISBN 978-1-77180-187-4 (epub).--
ISBN 978-1-77180-186-7 (kindle)

I. Title.
PS8645.E2175R44 2016 C813'.6 C2016-903325-2
C2016-903326-0

This is an original print edition of *The Recipe Cops*.

For Peter Satok, Tony Finelli,
and Andrew Bayley

# One

Looking back, the whistle of the kettle stood out as a harbinger of the unravelling of Sanford's life. That image, frozen in time, stayed with him: standing immobile, the telephone to his ear, and the surreal whistle of the kettle filling the air. A duplicate scene, occurring two weeks earlier, and informing him of the death of his mother, rose up once more.

The two telephone calls brought news, but the kind of news that comes at you from left field. On this occasion, as he stood there in his kitchen, the ordinary events of the previous five minutes repeated in his head on a closed loop: getting bread out of the fridge, putting a measure of instant coffee into a cup, filling the kettle, the kettle just beginning to boil. Then the telephone call, from the village doctor, announcing that Joe had died, almost a repeat of the events leading to the news of his mother's death. Now, the phone still to his ear, the connection broken, he stood there, dumped into a grey fog, struggling to believe the denial that was already in retreat. At the same time, he found that some corner of his mind, in what he supposed later to be a sort of defence mechanism, was busily engaged in a bizarre and meaningless juggling of immediate events on the calendar. As if a few changed appointments could somehow erase such a loss.

Saturday morning. Ten thirty. Barely an hour and a half previously, according to Dr. Hanley, Joe had died of a heart attack. He had been just four months past his sixtieth birthday.

Turning off the kettle, Jim Sanford experienced an odd sense of unreality and disorientation, not really knowing what to do next. He called his boss at home and said that he would need a few days off, but at the same time was shocked at a brief jab of concern that his schedule of work would be interrupted at a critical time. A palpable flow of sympathy returned immediately from the telephone, along with the offer from Stephen Maxwell, his boss, to take as long as he needed, that he knew how close Sanford had been to Joe.

Joe.

The man Sanford had known since early boyhood. A personal icon at every stage in his life. Next to his mother, the person he had known longest and best.

His mother.

Sanford had just about come to terms with her recent death. He had found himself looking forward to spending what he had hoped would be a healing four days at Joe's place, something that he and Joe had agreed to less than a week ago. Joe had seemed uncharacteristically cagey in making the arrangements for that visit, and that had puzzled Sanford somewhat.

What he felt at the moment was an expanding numbness, and an absurd flutter of fretting about what this would do to his schedule for the day. But Sanford knew that this also was just a defence mechanism, that the real pain lay ahead, that the two wakes of grief, for his mother and for Joe were converging.

As Sanford drove the two and a half hours from Toronto to Stanley Falls, the significance of Joe's death that morning unfolded in stages, pushing back other concerns, and eventually banishing them altogether. Joe. Gone. The blunt monosyllables kept hammering in his mind. Sanford had visited Joe many times as an adult; they had talked about the years of Sanford's youth, and Sanford always hoped that he had made Joe aware of what Sanford owed him, not that this was a debt that could ever be repaid. And it wasn't something that could be acknowledged openly; it had to be approached obliquely, subtly, by recounting the past in stages, and as a shared experience. But without having it out in the open, in what would have been gauche and embarrassing bluntness, Sanford felt beset by doubt that he really had thanked Joe properly, had made it clear what gratitude and love he felt, for the breadth and strength that his years in Joe's company had helped to build. Perhaps this was just part of the essence of generational indebtedness: that the best of the older generation regarded this stewardship and guidance as an unconditional duty delivering back its own reward, that the best of the younger generation saw it as the most noble altruism, and that in reality there was little common ground for these two to embrace. Perhaps the "pearls before swine" aspect of youth, recognized too late, if at all, by those who once had been young, was just one of those brutal facts, as in the notion that the teenager is an invention whose sole purpose is to rupture the child-parent bond, whatever the force required and whatever the hurt delivered.

Before the loss of Joe was able to crowd out everything else, Sanford fretted yet again over his own family, such as it was, or such as it had been. His marriage to Helen remained in his memory as a halo of delight, undimmed and unsullied even by the subsequent slow decline, his own increasingly panicky efforts to halt that decline, the unbelievable revelations, and then the final explosive rupture. And now, here he was, at the age of thirty-seven, his career in full bloom, but his family in tatters, and a past now devastated by two sudden deaths. In his mind, there were two strongboxes that held the brightest images from his marriage: the months of joy with Helen before and after their wedding, and the radiant gift of his daughter, Julia. But thoughts of his mother and of Joe were pushing these images aside.

His trip to Stanley Falls two weeks earlier had also been on a drop-everything basis. The details of that trip were a set of sharply etched stills that somehow blurred into one another. His overall recollection of it was one of being numbed by the blow of losing, suddenly and unexpectedly, the anchor from his boyhood and youth. The present trip brought all that back again, from its own separate alcove of pain, regret, and loss.

At that time, he had dealt with two tasks. The first of these had been to wrap up his mother's financial affairs, something that he was able, somehow, to work through mechanically, in a state of disconnection. The paperwork that laid out his mother's estate was simple and straightforward, but he had the strong feeling that she was there, in front of him, filling his senses every time he opened the folder of documents. Her neat and delicate handwriting, her essence that rose to him as a scent from the pages he worked through, the little notes stuck to the documents at various points, expanding on a detail, or giving a wisp of context, these all exuded her love and concern, and he could feel their touch, as gentle as a feather but as strong as a carpenter's vise.

It had taken him four days to go through all her things. He set aside and retained all her papers and photos, and the large diary she had kept for most of the past twenty years. All her clothes he had packed into boxes, and although he would ask her friends in Stanley Falls whether they would like any items, most of her clothes would go back to Toronto to be given to charities. She had kept a few items that she valued, and he decided to keep them all. The most important of these were the Br'er Rabbit mug and bowl from his early childhood and the several pieces of good china she had cherished. He also decided to keep most of her cooking implements, all of them old and solid, embodying a quality that was the hallmark of a bygone day. The furnishings in the house he had decided to keep, and this flowed from his decision not to sell the house, but to retain it and offer it for rent. His mother had been a neat and orderly person, and there was little that needed doing to the house. But Sanford had hired a few locals to replace some of the trim, to give a fresh face to the maple flooring, and to repaint the house, inside and out.

The second task concerned the house itself. It took little effort for Sanford to make it generally known that he wanted to rent, rather than sell, his mother's home. This had not been an easy decision, but it was far less painful than having to live with the thought of the place being bought and gutted by a stranger. His entry onto this path was eased by the offer from Anne Ferguson, a long-time friend of Sanford's mother, to be temporary resident in order to keep an eye on things, an offer that Sanford had accepted right away.

He entered Stanley Falls and drove straight to the office of the village doctor, Doctor Hanley, who gave him an account of what had happened. Joe had called Hanley at about ten fifteen, clearly in distress; Hanley had gone to Joe's place straight away; he found Joe unconscious on his kitchen floor, and although he did what he could, by the time the ambulance arrived Hanley had already pronounced Joe dead. Hanley offered Sanford his condolences, and then there unfolded that awkward encounter between those bereft of the power to do anything that can help, and those for whom the only help is time and grief.

Leaving Dr. Hanley's office, Sanford drove to Joe's place, less than a kilometre distant, and at the sight of the house the talons of loss took their first real grip. Joe's house was the same magical spot that had wreathed Sanford's youth in swirls of quiet love. The wood siding of the large, rustic house was immaculate – dark green paint and a tasteful *maquillage* of white trim joining forces to project a welcome that was at once strong and enfolding. The three large oaks in front of the house dared any trouble even to think of entering. A closely planted row of spruces, like a line of rugby forwards, so close together that they were almost interwoven, stood to the right of the path leading to the front door. Sanford expected, and could hear even now, the indeterminate number of birds that always called this thicket their home, serenading anyone who was listening. To the left of the house, and flowing in a graceful centrifugal arc that partially encircled the small log barn tucked away about eighty metres behind the house, stood the familiar stand of pines, displaying that odd wisdom of mature trees, and uttering a quiet susurrus, calming, reassuring, and as clear as the voice of the turtle. Joe's car was in the garage. The grass was carefully trimmed.

Sanford knew the same would be true inside. He walked up the drive, as he had done virtually every day of his boyhood. Entering the side door, he went through a small vestibule, then into the large kitchen, the place where Sanford probably had spent at least half the hours of his free time before the age of fifteen. As always, it was immaculate and inviting. Delightful patterned curtains graced all the windows. Rows of colourful china storage jars sat beneath a small choir of pale maple wall cupboards. The room exuded Joe, was the very essence of one part of Joe, and the talons clenched more tightly.

He quickly moved through the familiar rooms: the scullery where so many times he had washed his hands and gardening tools, and where the indoor pump sat, its rustic utility and old-time practicality always bringing a smile to his lips, but also its sheer permanence continually renewing a promise to deliver clear, cold, delicious water from the thick limestone beds sixty feet below; the den, where Joe spent a lot of his waking hours; and the lovely comfortable pantry off the kitchen. Sanford then took a quick tour outside, returned a smile to the trellis of roses dozing in the sun, passed through the pergola festooned by purple and yellow clematis, and then gazed at one of Joe's great joys: the large, well-organized, exquisitely manicured vegetable garden.

And Reggie.

Reggie, a handsome Setter-Labrador cross, stood outside his kennel. The kennel sat comfortably against the back of the house like a sentry box and faced the garden, which was surrounded by high deer-proof fencing. Reggie looked like a lost soul. Dr. Hanley had said that as the gurney bearing Joe's body was loaded into the ambulance and driven away, Reggie had raised his nose into the air and howled mournfully.

"Hello Reggie", Sanford said softly. The tail rose and began to wag. He was grey around the muzzle now, but showed none of that bent-legged look of the pain-ridden arthritic pet. This dog had been Joe's third Reggie – no Willie, Sam, or other interloper name even had a chance.

"I'll come back shortly, Reggie, then you and I can have a chat."

Climbing into his car, Sanford drove to the bank, where he knew Joe's will and other papers would be waiting. He nodded briefly to the bank manager, Mr. Cartwright, one of Joe's long-time friends, and he made a mental note to schedule a meeting with Cartwright soon. Picking up the package, marked and waiting for him, Sanford drove back to Joe's place. Back at Joe's, he fussed Reggie and fed him, made himself a cup of tea, and did a quick twenty-minute tour of the house and grounds, as the first step in an inventory of what, if anything, needed to be done. He was well aware of the size and nature of the task ahead: adjusting to the fact that he was now the owner of this country house and considering what he would be doing about that.

Based on this first quick inspection, Sanford came to a number of conclusions.

It appeared that almost nothing needed to be done, inside or outside the house. The entire property bore all the signs of being a labour of love that had responded in kind to the years of TLC lavished upon it. This made Sanford's job as simple as it could be.

Sanford called the bank, and was just in time, before they closed for the weekend, to book an appointment to see Cartwright first thing Monday to begin dealing with all the matters relating to Joe's will. He then unloaded his laptop from the car, since he wanted to send suggestions to his office the next morning on the projects he had left partly completed.

Starting the next day, Sanford would have to decide on the arrangements for Joe's funeral, but he felt fairly certain that there would be some instructions on that in Joe's will.

Finally, despite the fact that it seemed so crassly utilitarian, Sanford needed a plan, probably extending out over the next week or so. That would be about enough time to wrap up everything, package that corner of his life, and lodge it in storage. Part of that likely would involve the task of putting Joe's place on the market and selling it, a thought that occurred to Sanford as a reflex, without thinking what it would mean.

Sanford's thoughts were disjointed, barely formed – an odd mix of resolve and confusion. This was all emanating from two metaphorical boxes of personal freight – that fifth substance defining part of his inner life – and they had to be opened.

# Two

Sanford had grown up at the house across the street. Until two weeks ago, it had been where his mother lived. Seeing the small, neat structure once again, pale blue paint and white trim, just inflamed once more the pain of recent loss. His mother's smiling face, animated by an ever-present love and empathy, appeared again suddenly before his mind's eye. Aileen Sanford had lived for her son, and it was only in his late twenties and early thirties that Sanford realized the extent to which his mother devoted herself to him. His eyes stinging, Sanford let his gaze wander across the scene before him. Each aspect of this house and the attractive property it sat on raised a hundred images. It took a few minutes for him to regain control, and then he walked along the path to the back door, as he had done hundreds of times during his boyhood. A diminutive, pink-faced, spry, and cheerful woman stood just outside the back door and smiled reassuringly as he approached.

Anne Ferguson had been a long-time friend of Aileen Sanford. They had been through ups and downs together, and during Anne's recent trials Aileen had spent a lot of time with her.

These days, Anne insisted on being called Anne by friends and acquaintances, and Ms. by anyone else. She used the title "Ms." for want of anything better, but at the same time she very much disliked it. Ms. Ferguson was house-sitting for Sanford and for her departed friend Aileen, but while she was in the house, he regarded it as her domain, and private. So, before walking around the property, Sanford knocked on the door, explained why he was there, fended off the invitation to come in for what he felt might become a long chat, but agreed readily to spend a few minutes with her later at a garden table that held court amid a small irregular grove of apple trees to one side of and just behind the house.

Sanford took the time to stroll around the property, look again at the trees, the buildings, some favourite spots, and just remind himself of sounds and smells. These things all passed before him one at a time.

First was the Air Attic – a large, roughly cubical boulder, but a tricky place, located between a wild gooseberry bush and a nasty clump of poison ivy. Sanford had spent a lot of time there as a boy. The top of it was large and flat, large enough for him to lie down and stretch out completely without feet or hands hanging off any of the edges. Once up there, he was invisible. But there was only one way up: pull yourself up onto a narrow ledge at the back, hug the stone and work your way along the ledge until you reached a second ledge. This ledge sloped upward rather steeply, but with care you pulled yourself up onto and along that second ledge and then scrabbled up to the top, about twelve feet off the ground.

Lying up there he could look straight up into Betty, a huge birch tree. It was Joe who called her Betty, short for Betula, which he said was her proper name. After Sanford had learned most of the alphabet, it took him a year to work out that Betty is shorter than Betula by only one letter. Betty was enormous, and stretched way out over the Air Attic, the gooseberry bush, the poison ivy clump; over the roof of his mother's small and rather shabby garage, where there were jars full of nails, their lids fastened by screws to the underside of a row of shelving, this being one of the things left behind by the father he could not remember and never knew. On the other side, Betty extended out over the large flat rocks where he would lie and read a few years later. The lowest branches on Betty were too high off the ground for him to climb, and anyway his mother said he wasn't to try. But high up in Betty there was at least one family of orioles every year. When he was younger, before he knew what they were called, he knew that he liked their black and orange jackets.

Betty swayed gently. Her branches moved across the sky in complex patterns. Many times, there would be fair-weather clouds drifting past, and this made things even more complicated, since it sometimes looked like it was either Betty or the Air Attic that was moving. He would usually notice this suddenly, get the feeling that he had started to roll, and grip small irregularities on the surface in one of those fits of slightly fearful excitement. What he could see from the top was his world. The birds looked down at him curiously. Every now and then a small strip of white bark would flutter down, and each spring his first chore was to clear the dead leaves off the top of the Air Attic. He could still recall his startled embarrassment when it occurred to him that maybe he shouldn't be looking up at Betty from underneath.

It seemed that the days then were hot, summers were languid and endless, there was usually a light breeze, and when a car went by on the road past his house, clouds of dust rose like phantoms, and drifted quietly over the Air Attic. The dust would settle in his hair and make it feel dry and wiry. Tree frogs sang throughout the summer and on into September, although nobody could explain to him why a frog would climb a tree, and why they never sang that way on the ground. He remembered concluding, by the time he was five years old, that older people were not very bright.

The Air Attic was his refuge, but he also had his work.

His work consisted of studying. The place where he worked was right next to a large pine tree that stood within a few feet of the kitchen window. As he worked, he could hear his mother washing dishes, or clothes, or kneading bread, and humming. The pine tree didn't have a name. Well, it probably did have a name, but Sanford didn't know what it was. Next to the pine tree was his flower garden, although his mother did all the work in it. It contained only marigolds, because they were his favourite plant. He did his work on the concrete path that ran along the front of the garden.

He studied the charcoal-coloured bark of the pine tree, and the honey-coloured drops of pine sap that oozed out of small cracks in the bark. The tree had its own smell, but most of all it had a gentle voice, and it sang to him. His mother described it as "soughing" or "sighing" or "whispering", but it wasn't any of these. He didn't study the marigolds, but they perfumed his work area with a strong, sharp, and somewhat sickly odour. He had long since become accustomed to the smell, and would have missed it were it not there. The main thing he started off studying was the concrete. If he poured water onto it after it had been warmed in the sun, it would hiss. He studied this hissing for a long time.

His work changed once he discovered the set of dark-brown, ribbed, Orange Crush bottles, the ones that had the Orange Crush label painted onto the glass. He had found them in Joe's barn, and there were about fifteen of them, every one of them perfect – no chips, no nicks, no missing bits of paint. When he wasn't using them, he wrapped them up in pieces of old sheet and stored them in a cardboard box under his bed. The focus of his study soon changed from the concrete path to the Orange Crush bottles and water. He had a small plastic bucket that would hold enough water to fill two Orange Crush bottles completely, and have a little left over. Using a funnel, he became expert at pouring water from the bucket into two of the Orange Crush bottles without spilling any at all, and then pouring that water into two other Orange Crush bottles, again without spilling any at all. He became adept enough that he could pour water back and forth between these two pairs of bottles repeatedly, without spilling any.

Other images, vivid memories, swept over him in waves.

Once more, he could see the cows, smell their warm, damp odours, hear them munching, moving about, uttering the occasional cough.

At Joe's barn, the cows were milked every morning. Joe had just two cows initially, then four, and although Sanford remembered several of the cows being retired and replaced by younger ones, the four always had the same four names: Clara, Cosima, Constanze, and Elsa. Each cow had its name burnt into a small piece of cedar that Joe had then fastened tastefully above each stall. Joe did a lot of wood burning. Each of the bins in the barn was labelled this way, and there were odd little signs all around his farm. Each day, at milking time, Sanford would walk to Joe's barn, hold out his metal cup, and Joe half filled it with milk from one of the cows. He was a bit afraid of the cows because of their size, but they always looked at him with what he thought were kindly eyes. Half of this milk he would drink right away, while it was still warm. The other half he would save for his breakfast. While Joe finished the milking, Sanford would go off to a hay bale, and sit there sipping his milk. He asked Joe once if the milk tasted the same from all the cows. Joe said he didn't know but that they could do a little test. Sure enough, the next morning Joe had four small glasses ready when Sanford turned up. He could no longer remember whether the milk tasted different or not, so it probably didn't. As he finished one cow, Joe poured the milk from his milking pail into a large churn and then moved to the next cow. At the end, he pushed the lid onto the churn, carried it out of the barn, and placed it on a wagon. He and Joe then hauled the wagon to the house where Joe did some remarkable things with the milk. Sometimes he would stay to watch Joe separate the cream and then make butter, but sometimes he had too much work to do. When it was time for Sanford to return home and get back to work, Joe would telephone his mother saying that it was time to pick him up at the end of Joe's lane. She would meet them, and walk him back across the road. He would then clean out and dry his metal cup and go to the Air Attic. Or he would collect the Orange Crush bottles he needed, and his small bucket, go out behind the house to the pump, which he could just operate, and fill the bucket with water. Then he would go to work next to the pine tree and the marigolds.

The sounds and the magic of the evenings in his boyhood returned to him again.

Behind Joe's barn, there was a small swampy area with bulrushes, and in the evening he and Joe could hear the frogs croaking. (These must have been water frogs, and different from tree frogs.) Beyond the small swamp there was a very large meadow. At the far side of the meadow, there was a poplar forest, and at the edge of the forest there was a creek. Some evenings late in the spring they could hear dogs barking far away in the direction of this forest. His mother didn't know whose dogs they were. Joe said they weren't dogs at all, they were wolf cubs playing.

Eventually it became too dark to see much, most of the birds stopped singing (except for the boring bobwhites), and the mosquitoes started biting, so he would go inside and to bed.

But the strongest and brightest image, standing in for a reality he still could not believe had been lost, was that of his mother.

He pictured her again: slim, sympathetic face, shortish hair worn in a plain, attractive cut, little or no makeup. Most noticeable about her were her eyes, brimming in empathy, always seeming to radiate deep, everlasting, unconditional love.

Sanford spent time at each of the areas around his former home that held something special for him: the Air Attic; the garage, now looking even smaller and shabbier than he remembered; his small flower garden and its guardian pine tree; the stand of unruly sumacs that had claimed rough ground behind the garage, ground that was unsuitable for anything else; the large vegetable garden, now gone to grass; the rhubarb patch and his mother's peony beds; and his large flat reading rocks. He now stretched out on these rocks again and for just a few seconds was twelve years old once more, among the familiar poplar trees, which uttered a happy collective chatter as their leaves fluttered like large chunks of tinsel. He was just coming out of this extended reverie when Anne appeared at the door carrying a tray that held tall frosted glasses of something fizzy.

"Come and sit, Jim."

The only times she called Sanford "Jim" were when there was something personal in the air.

While handing Sanford his glass of lemonade, and pushing a small plate of cookies toward him, Anne commiserated on the terrible and unexpected news about Joe, but her good humour couldn't be suppressed for long. Soon she was all smiles as she asked, in genuine interest, after his life and doings in the fleshpots to the south.

Before he could reply, she dived off into an account of a recent trip she had made to visit her daughter in British Columbia, and she rattled on happily about that for a few minutes. It was not long, however, before her conversation circled back to Sanford.

"But how are you? You've been hit by two terrible blows." She paused here, eyeing him solicitously, then resumed on a different tack. "How is your work? Have you done much travelling? And are you still leaving all those eligible women in despair?"

It became evident that she warmed to him, mostly in a motherly sort of way. Her matchmaking efforts were very low-key and done mostly on a reflex *pro forma* basis, but somewhere inside she nursed a small ember from *Pride and Prejudice*, a harmless and often quite appealing bias that some people seem prone to retaining once they have imbibed it. In Anne's case, her own life hadn't really worked out according to the script, since her husband, to whom she had been married happily, or so she thought, for more than twenty-five years, suddenly abandoned his successful woodworking, furniture making, and small building supplies operation on the edge of town, and flitted to Mexico with a twenty-eight-year-old secretary. In a late-onset attack of insanity sparked by his lovesickness, he had burnt all his boats by deeding his business and their house to Anne. She didn't hesitate to claim legal ownership, and after six months she sold their house in a neighbouring village ("too big, too draughty, too him").

Sanford had recognized that Anne was a feisty soul, but her colours were really nailed to the mast when Mr. Ferguson had crawled home begging forgiveness. "*Demasiado tarde, Jose*", she told him, explaining that that particular quantity of water was not only well and truly under the bridge, it had drained through lakes, seen the insides of several sewage plants, made mud for pigs to roll in, and was now resting in a quiet patch of the South Pacific. In short, he was told to *vaya con Dios*.

He went, but it was doubtful that he had God for company.

"Is everything okay with your house?" Sanford asked, if only to shift his thoughts to more practical, not to mention conversationally safer, areas.

"You mean *your* house, surely."

"Well, yes of course, it is my house, but while you're living in it I like to think of you as more than just a lodger."

"Yes, everything is fine with the house."

They finished their drinks and Sanford thanked Anne and then left.

# Three

There was nothing to be done on Joe's house – no repairs, no touch-up painting, not even grass cutting. Joe had remained on top of everything.

Joe had sold his cows a few years earlier. He did it reluctantly, but his reluctance was not because he was particularly attached to them; rather, as he had explained to Sanford during a visit, because it had been a routine of his life for so many years and it felt like he was being deprived of something essential. But he had wanted to get away more, and after daily milking was no longer a tie, he had visited Sanford several times in Toronto, and stayed for up to a week. Even so, Sanford detected that Joe quite often felt it had been a mistake to part from his cows.

Joe had filled his hours, he explained, by spending more time and more imagination on his vegetable and flower gardens, and by doing more writing. He still had a dozen or so other activities that kept him occupied and interested. Some of this Sanford remembered from Joe's visits to Toronto. But Sanford's most delicious recollections, the sensuous sepia-tinged memories, were from his early youth.

Seven-year-olds don't always keep good track of time, either as hours or months. Sanford could only guess that his recollection dated from late April. He had already used his wagon to pull a load of cow dung back to his family garden from Joe's barn. Some of this dung was spread around the patch where the rhubarb grew. He described this operation to his friend Murray, and after that whenever Murray was at the Sanfords' place and was offered lunch, he would always decline any rhubarb pie. The rest of the cow dung Sanford mixed with the freshly turned soil in his mother's vegetable garden. But before he did that, it was another of his jobs to grub out the weeds and grass that were just beginning to grow. Most people didn't like doing this, but he found it pleasant.

So, that year, and one can say it was late April for the sake of the discussion, he was helping Joe in Joe's garden. It was the first time Sanford had done this. Joe's garden was huge. It was located in a large area outside his back door. The path from the back door went along the left side of the garden in a straight line to the barn. This wasn't just an earthen path. Joe had laid down large flagstones to make a four-foot-wide avenue all the way to the barn. He said he did this to avoid having the path churned into an unpleasant streak of mud in the spring. This would always happen, he said, because he had to go to the barn at least four times a day. He carried the milk from the barn to the house on a large sturdy wagon. He also used the wagon to carry to the barn the bags of feed that were delivered to his back door by the tall gangly man from the feed mill. The feed mill man was called Grant, as Sanford recalled, and he said very little. In fact, all Sanford ever recalled hearing him say was "Yup".

The garden was enclosed on all four sides by heavy wire mesh fencing. The fence was tall, much taller than Sanford was then, and the fencing wire was fastened to thick posts set into holes filled by concrete. The distance between fence posts was four of Sanford's big paces. The garden was eighteen by sixteen fence posts. At first, Sanford thought Joe was just being neat. After all, plants don't need to be fenced in. But when Sanford watched him that day replacing one of the posts, he realized that nobody would take that much trouble unless they had to. First, Joe had to unfasten the fencing from the decayed post, cut off the old post close to the ground, break up the concrete around the bottom of the post, then dig out the pieces of concrete. It was a lot of effort, but Joe wouldn't let Sanford help. He said the tools were too heavy and that he didn't want Sanford dropping anything on his feet. After Joe hollowed out the hole where the old post had been, he set the new post in place, adjusted it for height, mixed the concrete that he needed, and then poured it into the hole around the post, while Sanford held the post vertical. He then fastened the wire to the new post so that the post would stand straight while the concrete hardened. That was really the first time Sanford had looked carefully at Joe's garden, and he was surprised to see how even, and neat, and tidy it all was. The posts were all the same size, height, and spacing.

Inside the fencing, the garden was divided into six large sections and one smaller section. One section had raspberry canes, a second was planted in asparagus, a third potatoes, a fourth lettuce and cabbage, a fifth different kinds of onions, and in the sixth was growing what Joe called root vegetables. The seventh smaller section was a herb garden. Along the side of the garden opposite the path leading to the barn, Joe had managed to encourage some blackberry canes to grow, and they now clung to supports a few feet from the fencing, over a span of three posts. Not far from these blackberry plants was a large patch of wild strawberries. Joe said that it wasn't worth growing tame strawberries; the wild ones tasted much better.

It was during that year Sanford also came to a realization. He realized that Joe could not possibly eat all this food by himself. Even if Sanford counted the times that he had lunch at Joe's place, it still couldn't account for the amount of food Joe produced.

One day Sanford looked at one of the rows and the seed package that sat like a hat on top of one of the wooden pegs. "Joe", he said, "you have thirty-six heads of cabbage growing here."

"Yes. Six more than last year."

"How do you eat it all?"

"I don't eat it all myself. I use a lot of it to cook the Lions Club dinners."

Joe explained, "I love cooking. I learned to cook many years ago, and it didn't take long before I realized that cooking with very fresh food makes all the difference. You might remember that I gave a talk to the students here in Stanley Falls about food, vitamins, and cooking, and I explained a few different dishes and how they came to be. Partly a history of cooking. Only a few of the students had any real interest. But it was about a week later when William McCauley came to see me. His son was one of the students at my talk, and he told his father how interesting it was. So, William went to speak to the teacher, Miss Roberts, who had talked to me afterwards, and had asked me eventually what recipes I used. I guess she told William that I knew what I was doing. Anyway, when William visited, he spent a lot of time talking to me about cooking, and he spent even more time touring my garden and asking how long I had been doing this. Well, eventually he wanted to know if I would be interested in putting on a special meal for a few of the members of the local Lions Club. I said no. He asked me again a couple of weeks later and said he wanted to hire me to do it. Fifty dollars plus the cost of the food for preparing a meal for eight. He kept asking me, and finally I said yes, but just this once. Well, it turned out to be great fun, and so I've been preparing one meal a month ever since for the local Lions Club. I had to expand the garden. It was a lot smaller than it is now, and now I do cooking on contract. And that's where most of these vegetables go."

This was a long speech for Joe. So, obviously he really was interested in it. But Sanford was surprised and a bit bothered by it all. Joe must have seen something in Sanford's face, because he asked what was wrong.

"I thought that only women cooked."

At this, Joe almost fell down laughing, but he stopped rather quickly when he saw Sanford looking puzzled and a bit hurt. As Joe quite often did, he treated Sanford as though he was already an adult, and told him about something called *mores*. "Women cook", he said, "because it's a form of convention. They're expected to cook, and men are expected not to cook. It doesn't make any sense, because men are as good cooks as women, once they learn how, but most never do learn how." He said then, with a somewhat different look in his eye, that the expectation that men won't cook becomes almost a rule in country areas, but that it's a little different in cities. Sanford thought that might have been the first time he was aware of a difference between country people and city people. He was also pretty certain it was the beginning of his dislike of some aspects of life in the country.

They stood back and looked critically at the new post they had just put in place. Joe asked Sanford to trowel the last of the concrete around the post, and to make it nice and level. He said they would let it set for a day, and then tomorrow they would plant some catnip around the base of the post.

"Why catnip?" Sanford asked.

"So that cats will be attracted and scare away or catch mice and rats. The rats like to dig in the compost heap."

"Doesn't that bother Reggie?"

"No. Reggie seems to know his job, and his job isn't to chase cats."

"What is Reggie's job?" Sanford asked.

"I rely on Reggie to scare off the rabbits", said Joe. "There are two groups of animals we have to keep out of the garden: rabbits and deer. Reggie might be able to scare off the deer, but I have the fence to keep them out, and I've made it high enough that deer can't jump over it."

They both gazed silently at the garden. The rows of plants were very neat, and those rows that had been freshly planted still had a little stake at each end and string marking the rows. The soil was dark and damp, and there were pieces of straw visible in the soil from the manure that

Joe used as fertilizer. Looking at the tiny green shoots coming up gave him a funny warm feeling. He thought about his marigolds, but didn't say anything about them to Joe, because Joe's garden was so much bigger than his own.

"Why is there only a third of a row of lettuce?" Sanford asked.

"Well", said Joe, "if I planted it all at the same time there would be a huge amount of lettuce to use all at once and most of it would probably go bad. So I plant a third of a row every three weeks. That way, I have a steady supply of lettuce all through the summer."

They stood there for a while, like two guys assessing a used car. Joe gave Sanford a sideways look. "I think you would make a good gardener", he said. "Shall we go in and look at the herbs?"

The herb garden was laid out in squares, each square being home to a different kind of plant. There were squares reserved for parsley, thyme, tarragon, rosemary, nasturtium, sage, fennel, chives, mint (carefully sequestered to one side), and a half dozen other herbs. Each square had a little metal stake supporting a sign saying what the herb was in that square. Sanford moved closer to look at them. Some of the squares were empty, but some of them contained plants that were already large and growing. The sage was tall and woody and had dusty green leaves. The mint was bright green. The chives were small spears coming out of clumps in the ground. The thyme was a mass of twisted small twigs, and their little green leaves were just beginning to peek out of the undergrowth.

"What do you use the herbs for?"

"Ahhh!" Joe said, and the excitement in his voice made Sanford look up at him. His right hand was up before his face, he had his fingertips pulled together and was looking up at the sky. In that moment, Sanford saw a different person. In fact, Sanford thought it was just then that he realized that Joe was not just his nice neighbour and friend. He was someone who knew a lot more than Sanford had realized. Indeed, he was different from all the other people Sanford knew. In a very important way, it was evident to him that Joe was someone he had to get to know much better. Looking back, Sanford remembered the occasion clearly, but was no longer sure that it was just childhood memory. He felt that it meant as much to Sanford the man as it had to Jim Sanford the boy.

Joe continued to gaze at the sky, as if looking for something. "Let me count the ways", he said.

Joe turned to Sanford and said, in words that Sanford didn't understand, even though he knew they were significant, "Food is a great artistic delight, as well as an aesthetic pursuit, a backdrop for friendship, a condiment for discussion, a whetstone for intellect, and the ultimate bond between mind and body. And herbs help to extend the limits of all those dimensions."

He suddenly shook his head, and looked slightly confused and embarrassed. "Or in other words", he said in a more matter-of-fact way, "herbs make food taste very different, and are one of the reasons why life is worth living."

On a whim Sanford said, "Will you teach me about herbs, Joe?"

At that, Joe broke into a huge smile, and said "Okay. But first we go inside and wash our hands. I don't want your first memory of chives to be the smell of cement dust or cow dung." So, they collected the tools and took them all inside, then scrubbed their hands over the big metal sink in the scullery, and spent the next hour crushing and smelling the leaves and twigs of Joe's herbs.

This had all come back to Sanford so vividly, and so much intact, that it was almost as if Sanford had gone back there and was physically with Joe once again, reliving the entire scene.

Shaking off this reverie, and feeling more than a little pang of sadness precisely because the man at the centre of the reverie, Joe, was gone, Sanford sat down at Joe's desk and began to get his thoughts in order. He needed a plan for what had to be done over the next week or so. The main item coming up was Joe's funeral, and he needed to check on whether Joe had specific requests for that. But there were quite a few small things: placing obituary notices in a number of papers, making arrangements to pick up Joe's mail, checking his correspondence and seeing who needed to be notified, seeing whether any particular items from the will needed to be dealt with, and starting the whole business of selling Joe's property.

Picking up a pencil, he began.

# Four

Joe's will was in a sealed envelope.

Sanford hesitated to open it, because he had an absurd feeling that until he did that there was some slight hope that Joe was not really dead, some slim chance it was all a misunderstanding, and that Joe would return from the hospital, or from wherever…

He slid his finger beneath the envelope flap and pronounced Joe dead.

The will, which was not a thick document, was accompanied by a letter.

*My dear friend Jim,*

*Since you are reading this, I am dead. As I told you many times, the thought of leaving behind all the extraordinary things on this Earth, of leaving the acquaintances who have provided such a varied backdrop to my existence, but mostly leaving my close friends, and especially you, Jim, and the thought of the grief and upset this will cause, that thought has been hard for me to bear. But as you read this I am not in a position to worry about that any longer. All I can do here is give you my blessing as you carry on. As I write this, and as I think ahead to the moment of time you are in now, I can say that giving you my blessing is an easy thing to do. Easy, because having watched you grow through an inquisitive youth, through a late adolescence that was certainly unsettled in some ways, but then transform into a confident, capable, caring, educated, and fully aware man, not only able to stand on his own two feet, but capable of bearing almost any burden – well, this has been for me a source of the deepest unutterable joy and pride. I am prouder of you, Jim, than I would ever be able to express, and when I think that I might have played some role in that, I am prouder still. Go with your god, Jim.*

*The rest is details. I have arranged my papers and my affairs with you in mind. If you are reading this in what was my house, all that you see around you is now yours. Some traces of my life are in the papers in my various cabinets, and the pages attached to this letter provide what I think is the best path for you to take in going through that material.*

*Some of what you will find represents my own striving toward some of my life goals. I ask you to consider all those documents carefully. I am not interested in a legacy, which would be meaningless for me now anyway, but I put my heart and soul into these things, and they might have value for others.*

*Some of what you find will be disturbing, I have no doubt, but I ask you to consider that nothing I have done relating to you was done in any cavalier fashion, or without a great deal of thought. Whether I have done the right things, and how you judge what I have done, that is for you to determine.*

*Finally, I beseech you to take full account of the actions of the one person for whom you always meant the most, more even than life itself: the woman who raised you – Aileen Sanford.*

*She is a secular saint, and my regard for her has always been unbounded.*

*I hope you remember fondly, as I have done often, my cows, the time we spent milking, how Reggie made us both laugh, the hours we spent in my garden, in my scullery, listening to night sounds, reading, and most of all the time we spent in our little sylvan glade. These were some of the greatest shared joys.*

*I hope you can carry on with a fond remembrance of these things. I hope they will be a talisman for you, as they have been for me. I wish you a life full of intellectual, artistic, and professional fulfillment. I wish you humility before the world's riches. I wish you love.*

*Live a good life!*

*Your friend always,*

*Joe*

Sanford knew that he would return to these words again, many times. Some of them were enigmatic at the moment, but knowing Joe he was sure that everything would come into focus and it would all harmonize.

There were twelve pages of single spaced typed notes attached to the letter, but Sanford had to go for a walk after reading Joe's letter. It was Joe to the core. Pragmatic, caring, generous to a fault, scrupulously faithful, but really a romantic at heart. Heart. Noble heart. *Now cracks a noble –.*

Wiping his eyes, Sanford rose from Joe's desk and went outside. It was a beautiful day, waning but still beautiful. The birds were in throat, and the pines were whispering their eternal message of hope, the wisdom of trees.

There were some important immediate things to be done. He fed Reggie, and spent some time roughhousing with him. He looked over Joe's immaculate vegetable garden. He walked all around the house. Only then did he go into the "sylvan glade".

This glade was concealed within the same crescent of pines that he had known since he was first able to walk. The pines in turn were surrounded by a rabble of chokecherry trees, and together they formed a hideaway of which there was no external hint. Pushing through the chokecherries, which were much thicker now than he remembered, he entered the cool shaded area within the pine grove. It wasn't far to the clearing where the great table sat. King Arthur's rectangular table.

Sanford remembered the sketches Joe had produced, for an altar stone, a chapel, a cathedral, a shrine, a meeting spot, in the middle of the pine grove, and now here was the real thing once again. Although having the pieces of stone quarried, shaped, and brought to his house had taken weeks, Joe had had them put in place in one day. But then they did consist of only five pieces. He still remembered them sitting on pallets in Joe's driveway: large, beautiful, gleaming chunks of limestone, but looking almost like marble. They projected such an other-worldly aura that Sanford recalled being hesitant even to touch them, but when he did they offered a smooth, slightly irregular surface, covered in fine dust, having an Olympian coolness, seeming to represent time immemorial and a strong, simple, spiritual essence that easily outdistanced what he became aware of later as the confined trappings of conventional religions.

When they were finally assembled and in place, they spoke to Sanford even more strongly of radiance and power. Two very large squat blocks of stone rested in the clearing, about three feet from each other. A third piece of stone, about ten feet long and eight feet wide, a huge slab about ten inches thick, sat atop and overhung both the two squat supports. The fourth and fifth pieces of stone were solid benches placed on either side of the long dimension of the slab. Joe and Art Currie, who owned a heavy-duty front-end loader with forks, had previously identified a way into the pine grove that could accommodate, with some difficulty, Art's loader, and after preparing the ground to support the weight, they had brought in and placed the stones. Once these stones had been placed, they weren't going anywhere, and King Arthur's rectangular table in its sylvan glade was an established fact.

Sitting on one of the bench stones, something Sanford had not done for a while, and feeling its hard refreshing coolness, caused memories to flare up, and he could taste once again the hard-boiled eggs, the cheese, the homemade bread, and the raw carrots and celery that Joe would bring here for their lunch.

How many hours, days, they had spent here! How many times they had shared a meal here! What things they had talked about! What visions Joe had planted in Sanford's young mind! What love of nature, of learning, of discussion, of close and exacting inquiry, of the world's great vistas that awaited, of friends and friendship, and of literature and reading Joe had kindled in him! How much he owed that man! How inadequately Sanford had thanked Joe!

Snatches of Joe's letter fluttered behind his eyes. "A late adolescence that was certainly unsettled in some ways" – that made Sanford smile.

Sanford had always loved reading and studying, a legacy of Joe's informal training, which was nonetheless just about as rigorous as it could have been. Partly as a result of that, Sanford had sailed through his final year of high school at the top of his class. His teachers had great academic hopes for him, so when he told them that he wasn't going to university the following year, they were shell-shocked. One at a time, one after another, they took him aside.

Why on Earth would you not go to university next year?

Because I want some experience in the real world.

But you can get as much of that as you would ever want after you graduate.

Yes, of course I could, but it's not the same.

Why? What's the problem?

There's no particular problem. I just don't want to go into a hormone pressure cooker right now.

You think that's what university is?

That's what it can be, if one doesn't take steps to avoid it.

But you're aware, aren't you, that students who don't go straight to university run a grave risk of never going at all?

Yes.

Why would you think you're any different?

I'm not going out into the world just to get my hands on a lot of cash.

They failed to wear him down, and lapsed into confusion and despair.

Sanford had what he considered a normal adolescence, although looking back he had revised that view slightly, later on. Out of school, he had had male friends – Murray, Ron, Claude, David – whom he played hockey with in winter, swam with in summer, went to Scouts with. But in school, he was something of a different person, studious, not without humour, but not given to giggling, sniggering, and generally foolish behaviour. In fact, the only person he spent time with in high school was Jane, and they were considered, outwardly, an ideal pair. She was fair, medium tall, had an attractive oval face, long sandy-coloured hair, a slender build, a beaming smile, and an engaging but somewhat prematurely adult personality. This contrasted to Sanford's six-foot-plus height, curly black hair, dark eyes, solid physique, friendly but slightly impatient outlook, and skin that looked perpetually tanned. Jane's grades came in just below Sanford's, but they found in each other early versions of intellectual soul mates. Jane had no interest in amorous affairs, since she was an ace in mathematics, wanted to be an academic mathematician, and felt there was no time to waste on frivolities. All that would come later.

Sanford left high school, and almost immediately lost contact with everyone except Jane, but even contact with her was sparse or sporadic, and eventually petered out. He later described his next four years as leaving a band of sweat all the way across Canada. He worked in a small fish plant in Newfoundland, drove an iron ore truck in northern Quebec, spent six months working in a nickel refinery in Sudbury, worked various restaurant jobs in Winnipeg, was a dogsbody helper to a professional photographer in Saskatoon, collected garbage in Abbotsford, and then spent a year and a half working the oil fields in Alberta. A little more than four years after he had left high school, he bought a ticket back to Toronto, spent three days with a human resources consultant, and armed with a professional CV and a plan for the next ten years of his life, he began knocking on doors. Within two weeks, he had landed a job at a small engineering firm. The manager who had hired him was surprised at his lack of academic qualifications but greatly impressed by his understanding of the working world. The foreman who had grilled him offered the lament "if only the people who have worked here ten years could do what that kid can do". He arranged to start work ten days later, found himself a place to live, then spent six days in a memorable homecoming with his mother and Joe. They had been the two people he had corresponded with regularly, every two weeks, during all those four years.

Once Sanford began working, he made regular weekend trips to Stanley Falls to visit his mother and Joe, but at work he also activated his long-range plan. He worked like a demon, took all the courses that were available through the company, and within a year he had begun work that would lead a few years later to him being awarded a degree in engineering.

Sanford must have spent at least half an hour lost in reverie seated at the great stone table, but then stirred when he realized it was early evening, and that he would need to eat and get a good night's rest, because he had to tackle a full agenda of small tasks in the morning. Rising from the bench stone, Sanford returned to Joe's house, checked that there was more than enough in the fridge to put together a good meal for himself, then glanced through the twelve typed pages that accompanied Joe's letter. There was a list of documents identified, grouped by subject, and opposite each item there was a location specified in one of the cabinets in Joe's den. Sanford looked into the cabinets for the items that Joe's notes indicated were the first he should tackle. Everything was clearly labelled and in perfect order. He pulled out a few of the documents and looked through their initial pages. Joe's voice leapt off the paper and directly into his head. The material had all the arresting interest that every discussion with Joe transmitted, and while he looked forward to reading all the material closely, there was also an ambivalence, a resistance. Because these things were just a shadow of the Joe who was no longer there.

This brought back thoughts of his mother as well. Hers and Joe's deaths were oddly similar, she suffering a stroke, he a heart attack, both fatal within minutes, separated by just two weeks. Just as he had done now, he had returned to Stanley Falls then in response to a call saying that his mother had died. One of the managers in the local supermarket had heard a clatter of tins falling from shelves, went to investigate, and found her lying on the floor. She never regained consciousness and was dead within fifteen minutes. That had been June 17, a date he wouldn't forget.

Her affairs had been far simpler, but they showed signs that Joe had had a hand in helping her with the paperwork. Her death struck Sanford hard, perhaps not surprisingly, because of their closeness, and because the death of a mother not yet sixty is difficult to come to terms with. She also had left Sanford a letter. It was simplicity itself, but just as dignified as Joe's in its own way, and Sanford could remember it word for word. Sensitized as he was by the gentle and noble statements in Joe's letter, tears came to his eyes as he recalled his mother's parting message.

*My dear and wonderful son James,*

*You have been the ongoing miracle in my life. My love for you, James, was sometimes so strong that it felt unbearable. Although each phase in your growing up was memorable, the day you became an engineering graduate was the high point of my life. There you were, a tall, handsome, vigorous man, and that was my happiest day. Because of you, James, I am the luckiest woman in the world.*

*I hope for you all the world's joys, and all the pleasures, rewards, and fulfillment that can come to an intelligent and sensitive human being.*

*Your loving mother,*

*Aileen*

Sanford closed Joe's filing cabinets, then sat there for a moment, in Joe's chair. The light of a withdrawing day mirrored his thoughts. He looked around Joe's study, at the few books on Joe's desk and in the small bookcase beside it, books that Joe kept close to hand, and that he had thumbed through in fondness.

Then Sanford rose, walked into Joe's kitchen, and began preparing himself dinner.

# Five

The grey precursor of dawn was feeling its way past the curtains, pooling on the floor, climbing the angular shapes of door and window frames, and reminding Sanford that a day full of work was beginning. It was just after four thirty.

He rose, spent minimal time in the bathroom, fired up his laptop and rattled off the notes for his projects. After emailing these to the office, he had a quick breakfast and made an early start.

Sanford drafted obituary notices that would be emailed to the local paper, the Peterborough paper, and two major Toronto papers later that day. Sending emails that would initiate the legal arrangements to carry out the requests in Joe's will took a half day.

Making the arrangements for Joe's funeral was simple but took some time. Joe had wanted his friends to have an opportunity for a farewell. But he also had wanted the ceremony to be simple, followed by an immediate cremation, to have half his ashes interred in the village cemetery, and the other half scattered on the flower gardens in front of his house. That was a job that Sanford reserved for himself as a final personal favour for his friend.

Having finished these nominally undemanding tasks, Sanford felt drained. Not tired. Not sleepy. Not exhausted. Not weak. Just in need of something different, something involving a road ahead rather than the end of the road. Something linked to life.

The first thing he did was have a bit of a roughhouse with Reggie. Reggie was an oddly self-contained dog, always in the mood for the most vigorous activity, or the most sedate repose. The second thing Sanford did was to weed Joe's garden. A full weed of the entire garden would have taken the best part of the day, and Joe always said to him that that's not the way to deal with a garden. The comparable activity, and one that had as little chance of long-term success, was binge dieting. So Sanford spent about two hours in the garden, and the task of taking the care needed to distinguish weeds from vegetables, to remove the weeds without disturbing the crops, and indeed just being in proximity to the silent, undemonstrative, but enormous power of new life, was exactly the tonic he needed. Sanford collected the pile of extracted weeds, dumped them onto the compost heap, stretched in acknowledgement of muscles that had stiffened in complaint at unaccustomed exercise, and headed for Joe's house, now Sanford's house, to clean up. As he entered the back door to the scullery, Sanford caught himself whistling softly.

Although Joe had no longer had his beloved cows, and therefore no longer had made his own butter, he still used homemade butter right to the end, butter he had bought from a farmer who, he insisted on saying, lived about two miles away. (Joe was fully conversant with the metric system, but said that it belonged in the commercial sphere, and shouldn't be used to smear a tired and monotonous grey over our colourful inheritance of measures. When Sanford, wielding his metaphorical prod, asked Joe puckishly how far distant was his butter farmer in chains, he was chastened when Joe had answered, without hesitation, "about a hundred and sixty".)

Having cleaned up, Sanford cut a couple of slices from Joe's last homemade loaf, spread them in homemade butter, and took them into Joe's den. Diving into Joe's papers, using the roadmap Joe had provided him, would be a sober business, but not, he hoped, a particularly sad one. Despite his bucolic life, or – to reverse the usual urban condescension for things rural – perhaps as a natural complement to it, Joe was a complex and subtle person, optimistic in a way that was at once both elevated and austere, but also pragmatic, authentic, and earthy. In fact, Joe's view of life, which Sanford never convinced Joe to discuss at any length, appeared to be one of intense savouring of the present, while preparing as best one could for the vast range of future possibility, all of this informed by a deep awareness of the past. This outlook was summarized in a quote, from a now-forgotten author, that was pinned prominently above Joe's desk: *We never live the present as intensely as we might. We never prepare for the future as thoroughly as we should. We never drink from the past as deeply as we ought.*

Turning to the several pages of notes attached to Joe's will, Sanford read.

> *Jim,*
>
> *I have tried here to provide a sensible path through the mass of paper you see around you. I have given some thought to this, and the order in which I have organized things is, I think, the easiest and best, but of course you will do otherwise if that's what you choose.*
>
> *There are five areas in terms of priority.*
>
> *First, there is Reggie. Anne (Ms. Ferguson) has often said she would love to have Reggie. If the reality is different from the oft-expressed desire, please do what you can to find him a good home. He is a wonderful dog and has been a good friend.*
>
> *Second, there is the practical stuff, all the details of my property here, my investments, and so forth. All my files are arranged alphabetically. Among them you will find a folder labelled "Property" which contains a list of all the individual*

*files you will need to consult in order to deal with this. What you do with these items is your decision, but I have gone through them so that you shouldn't need to do a lot of digging and searching. This includes all my minor practical commitments, such as the Lions Club dinners, which now will have to be terminated. There are a few small bequests from my estate, but these are all listed in my will, and need no separate attention.*

*Third, there is my library which I have loved so dearly, and which you dipped into quite a bit as a youth. It's now yours, Jim. In my filing cabinets, there is a file marked "Library", which might be of some use.*

*Fourth, there is all my self-indulgent material. In the cabinets there is a thin folder labelled "Thoughts and Writings", and in that you will find a list of all the individual files containing things I have worked on and have felt, perhaps out of insufferable egotism, worth keeping.*

*Finally, there is a large file labelled "Personal". I ask you please to leave this unread until you have at least looked through everything else and decided in principle how you plan to deal with all that "everything else". This might sound odd, but there's a good reason for it.*

This note ended abruptly enough that Sanford checked to see if he had overlooked a page.

For two hours, Sanford busied himself at locating the files listed under Joe's third and fourth priorities. The first priority was obvious, and Reggie would receive all the care he deserved. The second priority was also obvious once Sanford had looked quickly at all the various individual files. Joe's record-keeping and organization were immaculate, and while it was clear that these second-priority files needed attention, dealing with them would be a matter of mechanics, given Joe's preparation.

The third item was a bittersweet surprise. The file labelled "Library" was almost six inches thick. It was a catalogue of every one of the approximately three thousand items in Joe's library. But the vast bulk of the file's content consisted of summaries, précis, reviews, or just sets of notes, one for each of the items in the library. Sanford took the file into the library proper, sat in the large wing chair that had been Joe's spot for reading, and began to leaf through the pages. The library was one of the largest rooms in Joe's house, it had no windows, and the entire available wall space was covered in floor-to-ceiling bookcases, all of them full.

About thirty years earlier, Sanford had sat in this same chair and read *Swallows and Amazons, The Wind in the Willows, The Railway Children, Alice's Adventures in Wonderland, Peter Pan, The Water Babies, The Little Prince*, and many similar books that made it easy to drift into other realities. Between thirty and twenty years earlier, while Sanford was in school and well before he had left on his four-year working odyssey across the country, Joe had led him, at increasing levels of rigour and under steadily more demanding expectations, through a comprehensive reading programme. Thanks to that programme, Sanford's high school literature studies were a breeze. His teachers recognized this, worked out that Joe was behind it, and in their turn placed greater expectations on Sanford than on the other students. Joe was impressed at some of the statements by his teachers that Sanford brought home, but more often these statements left Joe amused, disappointed, sometimes irritated, and not sure that Sanford's teachers knew quite what they were up to.

Joe's notes were a gold mine, but they were also overwhelming. Sanford felt overwhelmed by the care, diligence, and sheer effort represented by these notes. He was also overwhelmed by the memories they evoked. He set the thick sheaf of notes on the small reading table next to his chair, rose, and walked slowly in front of the shelves. There was more than a shelf of Greek classics – what looked like the entire extant works of Sophocles, Aeschylus, Euripides, Aristophanes – and several shelves of commentaries on Greek literature and Greek life. There were complete sets of Shakespeare (of course!), Shaw, Dickens,

Molière, Racine. Half a shelf was devoted to works by Goethe and commentaries on both works and author. Large sections were given over to poetry, to philosophy, to literary criticism. One whole wall was occupied by more modern standards, and many old friends smiled down at him: *The Riddle of the Sands, Berlin Alexanderplatz, Don Quixote, Doctor Zhivago, A Portrait of the Artist as a Young Man,* and many others.

Waves of nostalgia, gratitude, loss, and fond remembrance swept over Sanford.

Emerging from his bittersweet fug, Sanford returned to Joe's office and began making estimates of how much time he would need to work through everything. By late afternoon, Sanford had determined that he would need at least ten days to deal with all the items before him. He sent a message to his office, asking for and expecting to receive unhesitating agreement to have the next two weeks free for this task. By then it was time to think about preparing dinner. Sanford decided that the evening's meal would be Joe's long-time favourite dish, and one that he had helped Joe prepare many times. Everything he needed was in either Joe's freezer or pantry. By six o'clock, Sanford had a large pan of lasagne prepared and in the oven. Joe's selection of wines was nothing to be sniffed at, and Sanford chose a bottle of Brunello di Montalcino. While the lasagne was cooking, Sanford had another wrestle with Reggie, put down some food for him, watered the flower gardens and the herb garden, and generally lingered outside to watch the pines close in and embrace the sunset. The following morning would be occupied by a few practical matters easy to complete, including closing the books on Joe's arrangement with the local Lions Club, taking the first steps to having Joe's household accounts (telephone, power) changed to Sanford's name, and sending notes to Joe's correspondents and contacts.

Returning to the kitchen, Sanford poured himself a glass of the Brunello, prepared for his first meal of lasagne ever in this house without Joe, and returned to the great sheaf of notes that was Joe's summary of the contents of his library.

# Six

Not surprisingly, the amount of work needed to deal with Joe's financial assets was considerable, despite the effort that Joe had put into the files. Apart from three small bequests in his will, Joe left no suggestions for Sanford, but Sanford felt his friend's shade at his elbow as various thoughts surfaced in his mind. A donation to the local library was a clear contender, as was funding for an annual prize at the local school. A number of other possibilities came to mind without Sanford needing to make any effort. What was something of a surprise to Sanford was the size of Joe's estate. It wasn't enormous by current standards, but it sat at about $350,000, not including the value of Joe's house and land. Hardly trivial for someone having Joe's pastoral lifestyle. There were no notes or statements left by Joe on where this estate had come from, but the picture came slowly into focus as Sanford worked through Joe's accounts.

It was evident that a lot of Joe's net worth had been accumulated early in his life. Sanford knew that Joe had worked for about eight years following his university days, but he hadn't realized that a lot of this had been in the management consulting and financial areas. Joe's mental flexibility and potential to bend his mind to almost anything was not news to Sanford, but Joe having worked in these areas was. Joe's stint in business corresponded to the greedy eighties, and when Joe had cashed in at the end of that period it was clear that he had already amassed about two hundred thousand dollars.

But between the end of Joe's university days and those eight years of work, it became evident from his notes that there was a gap of two years, and Joe's records didn't reveal what had caused that gap.

It also became clear to Sanford, as he read on, that the farm had passed to Joe some time before he had begun working in the city, when his dissolute older brother, Archie, had finally drunk himself to death. Looking through the accounts and Joe's notes for that period, it became evident to Sanford that Joe had spent vast amounts of effort recovering the house and barn, which must have been seriously degraded. It also became clear that Joe must have commuted to the city during that work period, something that was surprising indeed. Joe had evidently worked like a fiend, and insisted on remaining at his farm, for a reason that wasn't clear.

Once Joe had given up the city and began living full time on the farm, there must have been some sort of activity to generate the small but steady income stream Joe's notes reported, and Sanford eventually determined that Joe had been busy writing (and selling) articles, reviews, some short stories, and carrying on extensive correspondence. All this came out of Sanford's first quick flip through Joe's files, after which he settled down to a more systematic perusal. But he had a specific schedule in mind while he did this, and at that point he was still hoping to wrap up his stay in Stanley Falls within two weeks.

Finding a real estate agent who would be interested in listing the property was not difficult at all. In fact, the very first agent he approached lunged at the opportunity and wanted to get together with Sanford right away. Sanford requested a meeting about a week away, giving him time to work through Joe's material.

Getting his head around the financial records, accounts related to the farm as a property, and Joe's personal financial situation was simple due to the superb way Joe had organized his affairs. Identifying the files that contained Joe's literary efforts, both published and unpublished, and setting them aside for more detailed review, also took relatively little time. By the end of the second full day working in Joe's den, all this had been accomplished. The third day was the day of Joe's funeral.

Joe had left a few brief instructions. Closed casket. Simple ceremony. Texts as indicated to be read. Music as indicated to be played. Immediate cremation after the ceremony. Gathering after the ceremony at Joe's favourite pub, Bend in the River.

Sanford had asked the bank manager, Mr. Cartwright, if he would lead everyone through a giving of thanks, and Cartwright agreed without hesitation. He and Sanford had gone through the elements Joe had suggested, a few changes were made, and then Cartwright insisted that he, Cartwright, be allowed to contact all the people who might wish to say something.

Sanford had hoped that the day of the funeral would not be dreary, and it wasn't. A brilliant sun beamed down onto the gathering. Although Joe was not at all religious in the conventional sense, the ceremony was held in the garden behind the small Anglican church. Unlike some countries in Europe, but common in Canada, there was no churchyard on the grounds of the church. But the garden behind the church was an oasis, enclosed by large maple trees, delimited by a colourful floral border, and having four trellises supporting roses, clematis, climbing hydrangea, and honeysuckle. This was where the farewell to Joe took place. Chairs had been set out in the open areas, and this worked well because the trellises made the setting attractive and appealing, by preventing a typical and unimaginative rectilinear layout.

Sound speakers were discreetly hidden behind foliage. There was no lectern or stand, and a wireless microphone allowed anyone who wanted to speak to do so from wherever they were most comfortable. Cartwright got the ceremony underway, and it was clear from the outset that he had met all those who would speak and had delivered to them his expectations. The programme came off flawlessly, and in graceful simplicity. Sanford could not have hoped for better.

Cartwright was an accomplished speaker. He began by stating in a strong and steady voice that this was a giving of thanks for the life of his friend, and without notes he summarized what Joe had meant to him and to many others.

Eight people spoke. The most affecting was the least articulate, but he honoured Joe's memory in words of such simple dignity that tears came to the eyes of even the most stoic. Sanford spoke last. His message was simply that Joe had been a beacon throughout Sanford's life, and remained so still.

More than a hundred people attended. Sanford managed to greet most of them individually. Joe's impact on each person, how they admired him, how they were sometimes overwhelmed by him, were the common threads. The lovely church garden was an ideal place to remember Joe, and many people stayed for more than an hour.

Then, Cartwright announced that the pace was about to change, that they were all going to Bend in the River to celebrate Joe in food and drink, exactly as he wanted them to. Sanford had arranged with Cartwright beforehand to have a generous food buffet laid out, one that he, Sanford, would pay for, and that the first round of drinks would also be on him, so that a toast could be made to Joe's memory, to his generous life, and to his legacy that resided in them all. Once everyone was in the pub and supplied a drink, the switch from formality to thankful celebration took less than a minute to complete. From there, it was a scene of recollection, laughter, and discussion that would have warmed Joe's heart. The celebration carried on for hours.

Sanford returned to Joe's place well after midnight. It had been an exhausting but cathartic day. On top of that, Sanford was tipsier than he had been in years. As a result, he stripped, crashed, and was out for the count within five minutes of crossing the threshold.

Having had the sense at least to down several large tumblers of water before falling into oblivion, Sanford awoke being able to apprehend a brilliant sunny day by means of a clear and painless head. He lay in bed listening to the familiar chorus of birds outside, but then a quiet "woof" reminded him that Reggie had to be fed.

Throwing off the covers, but rising slowly in case the clear head was just a cruel joke, Sanford went to the chest of drawers where he had placed his clothes the day he had arrived. The chest of drawers was not there. Uh-oh. Had he been far drunker than he thought? Looking around more carefully, he realized that he was not in Joe's bedroom. In fact, he had staggered into a spare room next door, which apparently Joe always kept completely made up, and ready for a guest, for some reason. Looking out the door of this spare room, Sanford quickly got his bearings, and recognized right away Joe's room, its door standing open, immediately to his left. Sanford also realized that the room he had just awoken in was far removed from the guest room he had stayed in during his many visits to Joe as an adult, a room that was at the other end of the house. Sanford was about to go next door to Joe's room to dress for the day, when his eye was caught by the large bookcase on the wall facing the foot of the bed.

Bookcases were not remarkable items in Joe's house, but the contents of this one were, and that is what had caught Sanford's attention. Almost all the books on these shelves were in Italian. There was half a shelf of books on learning Italian, another half shelf of dictionaries, phrase books, and grammars, and then the rest. The rest included some classics, some travel volumes, and a good number of nineteenth and twentieth century novels. There were well-thumbed copies of *Fiabe italiane*, *Le avventure di Pinocchio*, volumes by Guareschi, and two very dog-eared copies, one in Italian (*Il Gattopardo*) and the other in English (*The Leopard*). Sanford recognized a handful of names, but then passed on to other names that were blurry in his mind: D'Annunzio, Moravia, Bassani, Pirandello. Other, more contemporary names caught his eye: Calvino, Eco, Sciascia.

There must be almost two hundred books here, Sanford thought, not counting the reference volumes. How? When? Why did Joe accumulate all these books? All this was unexpected, and Sanford found it intriguing, mystifying. How could he not have been aware of such an interest, apparently deep, in Italian literature? Sanford pulled two books from the shelves, one in English and the other in Italian. They were *The Oil Jar and Other Stories*, and *Undici Novelle*. They were by an author familiar to him only in name, Pirandello. Judging by the use these books had seen, the frayed page edges, the notes and pencil markings, the interest had been deep indeed. There was no comparable trove in any other foreign language elsewhere in the house, at least not that Sanford had located thus far. Then came the greatest surprise of all.

Looking more closely at the copy of *Undici Novelle* that he held in his hands, Sanford realized that Joe's annotations in the margins were all in Italian. How could he possibly not have known this about Joe? Joe! One of the people he knew best!

Mulling over this odd discovery, Sanford washed, shaved, got dressed, then went out into a day of moist, pine-scented crystalline air to feed Reggie and run around with him. Reggie bounded about and yelped in pleasure. The two of them ran about the place, Sanford laughing, clapping his hands, and shouting, Reggie barking, wagging his tail as though it would twist off, going down on his front paws and daring Sanford to catch him, and generally behaving like a happy dog letting off steam. Sanford eventually caught Reggie, they rolled about growling at each other, the main result of which was that Sanford had to go back inside and change after he had fed Reggie and topped up his water bowl.

Having the funeral behind him, and most of the work on finances completed, Sanford set about finishing his first run through Joe's literary files. A few decisions came to him right away.

First, he would have the best of Joe's review and commentary pieces put together as a book, even if he had to fund it himself. There was breadth, astuteness, acuity, freshness, humour, intellectual frivolity, and substance there, and even a first sorting left enough material for a book of 300 to 400 pages. Second, he would prepare four or five of Joe's essays for submission to various journals, after passing them by a few trusted reviewers. Third, he would produce an appreciation of Joe and his life and work. Other options might become obvious as time passed. Although he promised himself that he would not stop and do any detailed reading during this pass through Joe's work, more than once he found himself five or ten pages into a completely absorbing essay or critique. At seven thirty that evening, he realized that he had read a quarter of the 90-page memorandum entitled "Portals in Literature and Life", and that he had become transfixed.

He closed the document, marked where he had got to in the total collection, and rose to feed Reggie and himself.

Joe's golden prose echoed in his mind, and he was stunned at the wealth of knowledge that glowed from the pages of Joe's essays.

After dinner, Sanford took a long walk, enjoying the sunset, listening to the emerging night birds, mulling over little phrases and sentences from Joe's work that had burrowed nooks in his mind, trying to reconcile how he had fallen so short of recognizing the literary store that Joe had been amassing, and wondering why Joe, whom Sanford regarded as a lifelong companion, had kept all this under a bushel for so many years.

# Seven

As often happened when in the country, Sanford awoke the next day before six o'clock, refreshed and in rhythm with the morning. The bedroom curtains glowed from the sunlight trying to force its way through and promised another brilliant day. But as Sanford lay in bed, preparing to rise, and reviewing his mental list of things to do that day, he was aware of whispering undercurrents. Ignoring these whispers, he rose, showered, shaved, dressed, made the bed, prepared and ate a full breakfast, and was seated at Joe's desk before 7:30. He had to finish his first pass through the rest of Joe's writing that day and then move on to the personal items that slept quietly in the third drawer of the grey filing cabinet.

Because of the previous day's exhilaration at reading Joe's material, Sanford was eager to work through the remaining items. The morning turned out to be far from disappointing.

He found poems, Joe's poems, and they blew him away. He found fiction, short stories that were stunning in the sophistication of their plots and the elegance of their execution. He found the outline of a novel and more than a hundred pages of notes for it. Oddly, and seemingly out of place, he found a very thick file that contained more than four hundred recipes, almost all of them carefully annotated. All this he would need to go through in greater detail later.

When he had finished, at just before 2 pm, what he had set out that morning to complete, he was convinced that two more volumes could be published, and that his own duty of reading and reflection, of coming to terms with a side of Joe that he barely knew, had hardly even anticipated, had just increased by an order of magnitude.

Taking a break before embarking on the last segment of Joe's files, Sanford went out once more to the sylvan glade. Brushing the fresh crop of pine needles from the table surface, Sanford ran his hand along the edge of the tabletop and one of the bench stones. Freshly quarried stone can have sharp edges, and he remembered Joe telling him about this, and about the work he undertook to round all these edges using an assortment of power tools. Feeling them now, he recalled how smooth they felt to his young fingers, as though they had been worn by centuries of water flow. The first day he and Joe sat down at their new retreat came back to him now in sharp clarity. Joe was proud, and excited, about their new meeting place.

"We need an inaugural meeting", Joe declared.

"A what?"

"Sorry. A first meeting. A kick-off meeting."

Sanford remembered recognizing that a ceremony of some sort was needed.

"We need something special", Sanford said.

"Yes", Joe responded. "What do you think it should be?"

Sanford remembered thinking about this for a few minutes.

"Do you remember when we welcomed the cows into their new stalls?"

Joe's eyes lit up. "Yes! And that's an excellent idea."

Joe had built new stalls when his complement of cows had gone from two to four. The two old stalls were creaky, saturated in urine, and the wood was beginning to flake away in spots. Joe had basically reorganized the layout of half the ground floor of his small barn, had built new feed bins at one end, rewired the place for lighting, and in the half of the barn next to the big doors where the cows entered and left, he had built four new, large stalls where each of the cows had plenty of room, and milking them was less an exercise in trying to compete with an 800-pound animal for too little space. During this construction, the cows had been housed in temporary stalls outside under a lean-to. Their first time into the new stalls was preceded by Joe "blessing" each stall and splashing a little milk over the fresh wood.

"What should we splash onto the new stones?" Sanford had asked.

Joe pondered this for a moment.

"It hasn't rained since our retreat was built", he said pensively, "which means that these stones have never seen rain, or any other water like that."

"But isn't it wet in the ground?" Sanford countered.

"Yes, but in the ground these stones had no real surfaces, they were just part of a very large block of stone until they were quarried. So, if we splashed water onto them, that would be our way of giving them something essential to life. What do you think, Jim?"

Sanford recalled clearly having puzzled that out. Just water? Ordinary water? But Joe was right, as usual. If somebody was dying of thirst, then water would be very far from ordinary. It would be special, important, something to give thanks for.

"Yes. Water is what it should be."

"Okay", Joe pronounced decisively, bringing his hands down onto the table stone. "Why don't you go and get your metal cup, the one you have your milk from every morning. I have my own special mug. We'll fill them with water from the pump. That water comes from limestone deep underground, so water going from stone to stone has a nice sound to it. Then we can pour the water over the stones here. Do you agree?"

"Yes", Sanford had said, beginning to become excited about a secret ceremony. Then he hesitated. "But, when we blessed the stalls, they had the cows' names on them. Shouldn't these stones, this place, have its own name?"

Joe had looked at him, then smiled suddenly.

"You're right, Jim! It should have its own name. What would you like to call it?"

Sanford had thought for a few minutes, then said impatiently, "I can't think of a good name. What do you think it should be?"

Joe looked up, and then an odd half-smile crept across his face. He began talking about the pine trees, and both he and Sanford looked around at them. They stood there, tall, stately, a graceful stand of trees, sweeping in a long collective arc through almost ninety degrees, falling just short of enveloping the barn in a soft, gentle embrace. Joe's voice dropped, so that Sanford had to strain to hear him, but even then he was unsure of the words. Joe said something about hills, and music, and warm nights, and he spoke several names, the reverence in his voice coming through clearly. Sanford listened to the trees, which were in turn, it seemed, listening to Joe, but then, breaking a relative lull, the trees around them uttered a peaceful but insistent whisper – a collaboration of winds and pines sounding like a drawn-out "Yyyeeeeesssssssssss".

"The trees liked that", Sanford said suddenly.

Joe blinked, looked confused.

"What you just said. I don't know what you meant, but the trees liked it."

Joe inclined his head, still somewhere else mentally.

"'The Recipe Cops'", Sanford said. "I think that's what you said. I don't know what it means, but the trees liked it. And they've been here a long time."

Joe blinked again. "Indeed they have. And their opinion matters. So 'The Recipe Cops' it is."

It took only a few minutes for the two of them to retrieve their cups, their chalices, and to fill them. They stood across from each other at the great table stone.

"This is something special, a special place", Sanford said. "What would you say about it Joe?"

Joe thought for a moment.

"I think, Jim, that it was a time to gather stones together, and that's what we've done. So, let's anoint our special place, 'The Recipe Cops'", and they both poured their cups of water over the stone.

Sitting now at the stone table, decades later, Sanford had the same ethereal feeling that he sensed back then. But now it was mellowed by years of Joe's company, uncounted numbers of conversations he had had with Joe, when Joe had suggested, proposed, guided, advised, and in general led Sanford out of the darkness and into the light, partly by walking him repeatedly into the seclusion and the shelter of this sacred little spot.

Reflecting back over Joe's literary works that he had skimmed through during the past two days, considering with delight but also a kind of astonishment the new side of Joe thus revealed, Sanford eventually returned to the house and to Joe's office after a break of almost three hours. There was one last set of Joe's files to review, then the difficult review phase of his work would be finished, and he could revert to a more measured process of dealing with the individual items, over time, and in some final and definitive way. The thought rested uneasily, because this would mean that his last act as Joe's friend would come to an end.

# Eight

Sanford read over once again the instructions Joe had left for dealing with his files.

Five general areas: Reggie, practical matters and Joe's financial estate, the library, Joe's writing, and the material Joe referred to as "Personal".

Priorities: Joe's request to deal with "Personal" last. It was now time to deal with the personal stuff.

The files Sanford needed were in the third drawer from the top of Joe's filing cabinet. There were six files altogether, and rather than being labelled using names or text, five of them were numbered. The sixth had no markings of any sort, but was thinner than the others, and contained something solid. Sanford opened this unmarked file first.

Inside, wrapped in multiple layers of thin white paper, was a piece of wood. It was a carefully cut rectangle of cedar, the edges rounded, and the rich wood scent rose into the room as soon as Sanford unwrapped it. *The Recipe Cops* was burnt into the wood. Sanford had never seen this artefact before, but by the feel and smell of the wood it had been made fairly recently. On the back of the piece of wood, a small card was taped and in Joe's handwriting stated simply "For Jim".

Beneath this piece of wood in the file was an envelope. It contained a single picture. The picture was of a young woman, smiling, appearing as though she were about to break into a laugh. She was leaning back, in a completely relaxed pose, against an expanse of white stone that looked like marble. There was nothing in the envelope or on the back of the picture to say who she was, or where or when the picture had been taken.

Sanford turned to the other files, which were numbered simply "1" to "5", and sorted them by number. He looked quickly through all the files. The files numbered "2" to "5" recorded all Joe's dealings with people in the village, although one of them contained intriguing correspondence between Joe and various individuals, including several of Sanford's teachers. Sanford began by opening the file labelled "1".

This file contained about fifty pages of notes, extending over a period of many years. Sanford settled in to read the notes. Each note was dated.

It was apparent soon enough that these were notes Joe had made on conversations he had had with Aileen Sanford, Jim's mother.

Joe's notes recorded discussions between Aileen and Joe on practical, financial, and personal matters. It was evident that Joe and Aileen had been confidants. Aileen had also confided her uncertainties, her worries, her insecurities, and many of these discussions had concerned him, her son.

Sanford could sense a slow anger growing within him. *Where the hell had my father been?* Sanford asked himself gruffly.

But Sanford knew very well where his father had been. His father, whom he knew only as "Harold", was a deadbeat. Sanford had no recollection of him whatsoever, although he assumed they must have spent some time together when Sanford had been an infant or a toddler. "Harold" was always off somewhere. When Sanford was old enough to ask, he would say to his mother "Where's Dad?" The answer was always the same: "He's on the road. He has to travel a lot for his work." By the time Sanford was six or seven, he no longer believed these statements, and he had become, by turns, indifferent to and resentful of his father. "Harold" apparently sent money home to Aileen, which was something, but hardly a substitute for being around.

The notes covered discussions throughout Sanford's childhood and early teen years. They fell away somewhat during the time Sanford was working his way across the country, but they never ceased entirely. Then, very recently, there was a change. The notes reported a change in Aileen's behaviour, her outlook, her equilibrium. They started just a few weeks before Aileen's death. Then they mentioned a disturbing visit to Aileen from a man called Charles Jeffers.

Sanford came to the final two notes.

The second-to-last note was dated just a week before Aileen's death. Joe had written the following:

> *Saw Jeffers' car pull into Aileen's drive. Jeffers jumped out energetically, grabbed a bag from the back seat, and went into Aileen's house. This time, I decided I would not wait to hear about things after the fact. I walked across to Aileen's house and stood beside the kitchen window, which was open because of the lovely weather. There were voices, not quite normal, but not raised in anger. Then suddenly there was an argument. I heard Jeffers say loudly, "Yes, you will!" There was pleading from Aileen, words that I couldn't catch, then she cried out. I had no choice but to intervene, and that ended the argument. Jeffers then left without a word.*

The last note was dated just the next day. Joe had written simply this:

> *The problem has been solved. Material no good for milk.*

The account ended there. Joe had written nothing further. The last sentence meant something, but the meaning came from a far distant past. The memory that rose in Sanford's mind was clear and unambiguous. Joe would muck out the cows' stalls every second day, and Sanford almost always watched. He was then far too young to lift forksful of the heavy dung and straw mixture, but he liked to watch Joe work. Whenever Sanford wrinkled his nose in distaste, Joe would almost always wink at him, and say through a smile "Material no good for milk".

Sanford sat back in bewilderment. Why did this statement appear here in Joe's notes? What could it possibly mean? Sanford rose from Joe's desk and walked into the kitchen. He crossed the kitchen and looked into Joe's bedroom. He went outside and looked across the road to the house where he had grown up, where Anne Ferguson now lived.

He felt cold fingers at the base of his spine. Something dark began filling his head.

It took a good hour before he had his answer. The answer was, initially, a horrific stench, and then a brown leather shoe. The shoe was on the right foot of a body that lay at the bottom of a pit about four feet deep.

There was a body under Joe's manure pile, a pile whose surface was now dry and shrunken, not having had cow dung added to it for at least three years.

Sanford had stumbled back to Joe's office as the afternoon closed in, where he sat, shocked and bewildered, trying to think it all through. A few things occurred to him almost immediately.

What about Jeffers' car?

Sanford shook his head, trying to clear the fog, trying to find a rationale to support the denial that was rushing in.

Joe wouldn't do something like that. Joe was one of the most civilized men Sanford had ever known. There had to be some other explanation. It couldn't be Jeffers.

But, if so, then just who was buried under Joe's manure pile? Indeed, why was *anyone* buried under Joe's manure pile?

Against Sanford's deepest resistance, and despite the fact that it was the very last thing he wanted to do, he went back to the manure pile. Dusk was settling by the time he had the answer. The body was dressed in a good suit. There was nothing resembling a wallet. Nothing that looked in any way like a scrap of paper. The stench was unbearable, and Sanford suppressed the reflex vomit impulse only by a supreme effort of will. The face was discoloured but the features were clear. It was a face Sanford would never forget.

What to do? What the hell should he do?

He covered the body again, and arranged the manure pile so that it looked natural, and the disturbed manure would take on a dried, sun-bleached, and undisturbed look after just a few days. Sanford then stumbled back to Joe's house, shaken and shaking.

A moment's thought convinced Sanford that this could not be reported. The implications of his taking such an action, of going to the police, became obvious immediately. There would be an investigation, and an investigation would bring out everything. His mother's memory could well be blackened. All the good Joe had ever done, all his acts of kindness and generosity would be swept away and replaced by the dark suspicion: 'Murderer'. No. Sanford was going to sit on this information and not tell anyone.

Besides all that, Joe could think clearly. If this was Jeffers, and if Joe had indeed killed him, he would have done it only for a very good reason, and he certainly would have considered all alternatives, such as trying to scare Jeffers off or reporting him. But there was no hint in Joe's notes on why Jeffers was suddenly paying close attention to and harassing Aileen. Without knowing the "why" it would be difficult to formulate an effective "scaring off" strategy. And as for reporting Jeffers? Joe probably knew, or suspected, that Jeffers would have been able to weasel away, while he had been alive, from any taint or accusation concerning dealings with Aileen. If, as Sanford was becoming convinced, the body was that of Jeffers, and if Joe had put it where it was, then Sanford needed to understand why Joe had done this. A very good reason would have been Joe becoming convinced that there was some dark intent on Jeffers' part in approaching Aileen. But Sanford felt that whatever such intent might have been, it probably did not involve something as straightforward as harassment or abuse. Most likely, there was something else going on, and he suspected that Joe had probably guessed what that something else was.

So, had Joe concluded that the only way to deal with the matter once and for all was to eliminate Jeffers? Looking back through Joe's notes, Sanford realized that there was nothing in the notes that would lead anyone but Sanford even to guess at the presence of a body, and to suspect what had happened. But there was more than enough for Sanford himself, Sanford alone, to reach the conclusion he had reached. Joe had left the message, clear and unambiguous, for Sanford's eyes only.

Why?

Sanford concluded that Joe wanted him to be informed, and not stumble into anything very unpleasant.

Sanford looked carefully once again through the file. He had missed nothing important the first time. The pages had been punched at the top and were held in the file by a brass clip. They were numbered, and no pages were missing. He lifted the pages and looked at the inside back of the file. Nothing. He turned the file over. There was a note on the back:

*Remember to show Elias Wilson favourite spot for reflecting.*

Elias Wilson had been dead for more than ten years, pre-dating all but about the final quarter of the entries in the file. More importantly, Sanford knew that Wilson had been one of Joe's least favourite people. They never spoke, and Joe would certainly not involve Wilson in anything as intimate as sharing a "favourite spot for reflecting".

What's more, Sanford knew exactly where that spot was. About ten miles from Stanley Falls, there was a quiet back road that skirted Eagle Lake. The road followed a gentle curve past the lake, and at a certain spot one could climb down from the roadside to a ledge that was just right for sitting and looking. This ledge gave a view, particularly stunning at sunset, over the lake and two small islands several hundred metres from the shore. At sunset, on calm evenings in July and August, these islands cast surreal and haunting images across the lake. Looking down from the ledge when the sun was still above the horizon, one was met by dark water – just there the rock cliff plunged straight down.

The water there was deep. Deep enough for a car to vanish without a trace.

# Nine

Sanford got no sleep that night.

It wasn't that he tossed and turned. He didn't go to bed at all. He spent the rest of the night poring over the files Joe had left him. And the following morning. And that afternoon, until he fell asleep at Joe's desk.

By that time, Sanford had gone through all the files, including the one labelled "5", a file which appeared to indicate that Charles Jeffers didn't exist. Everything in the file was oblique, probably to avoid any fingers being pointed anywhere, since the discovery of a body beneath Joe's manure pile as a result of any such pointing could have been disastrous for both him and Aileen. It appeared that Joe had used two or three independent operatives to try to track down Jeffers. Did Joe want to know who it was that he had killed because he felt remorse? Did he want to know just because he wished to unmask, if only for himself, the identity of a very unpleasant leech who perhaps had tried to attach himself, somehow, for some reason, to Aileen? Or did he want to know whether there was something else behind the whole episode?

All this caused Sanford considerable anguish, and he had to go out for a walk again to regain the quiet and equilibrium needed to come to some conclusion on what he had learned thus far from Joe's files. This time, he walked past Joe's flower beds in front of and to the left of the house, as one looked from the house toward the west. There were four flower beds, of different sizes and shapes, and Joe used them to different effects. In one bed Joe grew tall, exuberant flowers, like oriental poppies, hollyhocks, gladioli, and mullein, against a backdrop of forsythia that produced cascades of bright yellow in the spring. In another bed, he had planted low fragrant flowers, and these were dominated now by the marigolds. In a third bed, Joe had laid out a variety of climbing plants, each clambering up its own trellis or pergola. And in the fourth bed were what Joe called his "kitchen flowers" – dozens of pansies and nasturtium, whose flowers he used for decorating food; various pepper plants; and about a dozen sorts of annuals that were his cutting garden. Sanford recalled the number of occasions when Joe had cut some of these flowers, brought them into his kitchen, arranged them in vases, and stepped back wearing a huge delighted smile.

Half of Joe's ashes had been scattered on these gardens.

"What happened Joe?" Sanford asked the flowers. "What's going on?" And he shivered as the frightful image of that dead face rose up again in his mind.

Sanford's walk led him to the barn. It was scented of hay, grain, and large animals. But it was now also quiet and somewhat forlorn. The scents were subdued, missing the sharp edges that warm live fur exudes, and missing the ammoniacal pungency of excreta. Unlike barns made of timber frame and boards, Joe's barn was more log-cabin style, large hewn baulks fitted together carefully on their long dimensions, well caulked along these lines, solidly mortised at their ends. The interfaces between the baulks were filled, inside and out, by whitewashed plaster, forming long, attractive, horizontal white stripes against the weathered grey of the wood. Because of this solid and generally airtight construction, there would have been no continuous breeze through the barn, not a good condition when one is keeping animals inside for long periods, so Joe had installed a set of louvred vents, and these had kept the air inside clean and fresh, but always, of course, laced by heavy underlying animal odours. Even after all these years, Sanford's youthful memory of the place was fresh, vivid, and clearly defined. Walking to the far wall, Sanford examined the filled lines between the baulks. Even here, Joe's recent hand was evident.

The names of the cows were still in place, burnt into the short planks mounted above where their heads had been.

But outside, less than twenty feet away, there was something unspeakable, and Sanford could feel its black claws rasping at his thoughts.

Sanford's all-nighter was now catching up to him, and he knew that he would need to turn in early. Better, then, to get back to Joe's desk and carry on while he still had the energy and the focus to do that. By then it was late afternoon. Seated again at Joe's desk, he pressed on for another hour.

Sanford's eyes were beginning to sting from lack of sleep, and he took another break to select some vegetables and herbs from the garden for an early dinner. He had decided to make an arrabbiata sauce, full of life and flavour. He also took the opportunity to feed Reggie, who responded with his usual infectious enthusiasm.

Returning once more to Joe's desk, Sanford felt that he was in the home stretch, but it was now close to seven in the evening. Having skimmed over sections in Joe's notes, he went back now and read them more closely. There was a long section of notes that recorded Aileen's concern over Sanford's decision to put off university in favour of a few years' work, and Joe's assurance that "Jim knows what he's doing". Joe's notes related his discussions with Aileen on conversations Joe and Sanford had had on what Sanford would study eventually when he took a university course, and how Sanford was looking forward to all that. These, in fact, were discussions that Sanford remembered clearly.

He closed the file, rubbed his weary face, and hoped that spending time in the kitchen preparing his dinner would put some distance between his satisfaction at the progress he was making and the dark things he had just learned. But all he actually felt over the rest of the evening was a massive and ominous uncertainty.

# Ten

A modest helping of what Sanford was pleased to admit was a timely and welcome meal left him in better spirits. But it was the exuberant final minutes of an airplane running on fumes. In order not to be solitary for what was left of the evening before he crashed, he invited Reggie to join him on the front porch. Reggie displayed his usual apparent instant mood swing, by going from somnolence to full enthusiasm in less than a second, and they both walked into the house via the scullery, and through to the door onto the porch. The front porch was a comfortable space that Joe had enclosed in screening, and Sanford could sense the rage of hundreds of mosquitoes detecting blood but having their access to it barred. The western sky was a symphony of practically the entire visible spectrum. Reggie sat quietly next to Sanford, just the way a civilized friend of Joe's would be expected to do, and occasionally looked up to Sanford, in that canine way that spoke of life being truly good.

It took less than half an hour for the tank to run dry, at which point Sanford dragged himself to his feet, fighting off the tender and alluring clutches of Hypnos, first to lead Reggie back to his kennel and drape his mosquito netting over the frame that surrounded it, then to re-enter the house, batting away the last few bloodsuckers. He had just about enough energy left to brush his teeth and fall into bed.

The sun was already well up when Sanford awoke, feeling better, and at least having a sense of energy and purpose. After washing, shaving, and dressing, but before doing anything else, he called his boss in Toronto.

"Maxwell."

"Stephen. It's Jim."

"Ah! Jim! How's it going? Er, sorry, I mean how are you coping?"

"Fine thanks. Look, Stephen. I want to come into the office today" – a grunt of objection here that he ignored – "and make sure that all my projects are on track."

"There's really no need, Jim. I assure you that everything is in place."

"I'm sure it is, Stephen, but this whole thing is going to take a little longer than I expected, I'm afraid, and I want to make sure that there are no messes or screw-ups."

"Well, Jim, I think you're worrying about nothing, but by all means, come in and do what you need to do. How much longer do you think you might need?"

"Probably not more than another two weeks. I have the leave available, but I'm more than willing to take time without pay."

"Nonsense! I won't hear of it. Drop by my office when you arrive, which will be, I suppose, about noon?"

"Yes. About noon."

"Good! See you then Jim."

"Thanks Stephen."

Sanford's mind was oddly blank during the two-hour run into Toronto. Once he had arrived in the office, he reviewed his projects with the people who were subbing for him, went over contingencies, made sure that they would call him if any of the projects suddenly lurched sideways, found not even a hint of a problem in any of his projects, and was back on the road to Stanley Falls by three o'clock, just barely missing the rising peak of the evening rush hour. He spent that two-hour return trip thinking about his mother.

But not just his mother.

It was clear to him by the time he left the office for his homeward trek, that the trip had been completely unnecessary. His time in the office had added nothing. In fact, it had served just to puzzle and confuse the people who had taken over his projects. This was so evident after the fact that he was amazed he hadn't seen it immediately that morning and not made the trip at all.

He had made the trip to Toronto to avoid something. Another day reading Joe's files? Another day coming to terms with what had been lost? Another day of trying to make sense of, or perhaps just to ignore, what it was he had found? Another day approaching the tough decisions about Joe's property and belongings? It was really none of these reasons on their own; it was all of them put together.

Sanford drove mechanically, living within the internal silence and the unwelcome images that lurked in his mind. The lovely countryside, drenched generously in sunlight, drifted past almost unnoticed.

Stanley Falls was just beyond the next hill, which, when crested, brought the town gradually into view, and this was the origin of the stale local joke "Stanley Rises". As Stanley rose just now, Sanford decided that he wouldn't be stampeded by some upstart inner voice into dropping everything and going in search of – what?

Sanford pulled into Joe's drive at just after five that afternoon. The day had gone from bright, clear, and hot, to hazy, muggy, and even hotter, and it looked like a thunderstorm was on the way. There was, first of all, the enjoyably energetic romp with Reggie before Sanford fed him, then the preparation of a quick and dirty Caesar salad with herby grilled chicken slices, which Sanford decided he would eat on the screened-in porch. Going out to the back of the house first, he looked at Reggie, who looked back expectantly. "Come on, then!" Sanford said to Reggie, who bounded alongside without hesitation, and the two of them settled on the porch just as the first lightning began splitting the dark clouds to the south. Within minutes, thunder was booming around the sky, as though hordes of giant lumberjacks were felling monster trees. Reggie edged closer to Sanford's chair, and shivered a little less violently when Sanford reached down to scratch his ears.

"What do you think Reggie, hmmm? Did Joe kill Jeffers? Did he bury his body under the manure pile?"

Reggie looked up at him, wagged his tail uncertainly, and cocked his head the way dogs do when it seems that they're trying to work out something.

"I guess you wouldn't know, would you? You probably weren't there. But Joe might have said something to you. You look like the kind of guy who invites confidences."

Reggie groaned, licked his chops, and blinked.

"But it's a pretty drastic thing to do, isn't it? Especially if it was premeditated, and what else would it be? Surely Joe didn't have a plan in his head, ready to commit the perfect crime. Or did he?"

They both looked into the night, listened to the thunder, and pondered that one.

"And where did he do it, if he did it? It could hardly have been in my mother's house. She wasn't strong enough to be able to be complicit in something like that and then live with it, hide it successfully. What do you think?"

Reggie uttered a low "woof", and licked Sanford's hand.

"Well, I'm glad we agree on that."

There was another pause while they watched the sound and light show above. Reggie edged a little closer.

"And Jeffers would have been no pushover. If he had the street fighter moves that his phantom record might imply, then he would have been more than a match for Joe. But even if that supposition is wrong, even if Jeffers had no special training, to live the kind of life he seems to have lived, among the kind of people he dealt with … well, he most likely wouldn't have been a pushover."

"I hope that Joe didn't kill him, Reggie. But whether he did or not, the fact that it's almost certainly Jeffers' body under Joe's manure pile still leaves a lot of explaining."

This was a long bit of logic for a dog to navigate, even one as gifted as Reggie, and Sanford sat quietly for a minute.

"But, supposing that Joe did do it. It couldn't have been a crime committed on impulse. It must have involved just the right opportunity."

Reggie raised no objection to that.

Even for a situation like that, and Sanford had to admit he had no real idea what that "situation" might have been, murder is a drastic measure to take. Surely there would have been other ways to get around or dodge whatever the problem was.

"So, why –", Sanford's thought began, but then was interrupted by another.

"Joe must have been worried about something. Very worried."

A brilliant flash seared the evening, and the violent crack of thunder that followed almost immediately felt like confirmation by a higher authority that Sanford was onto something. Joe's primary worry would have been for Aileen. It was doubtful that Jeffers would have had any interest in Sanford, otherwise Sanford would have been the target right from the beginning.

Reggie huddled against Sanford's leg, shivering violently, evidently concerned that whatever caused all the flash and racket had a bite even worse than its bark.

Sanford patted the side of Reggie's head in reassurance, shunting aside another reflex attempt by the manure pile horror to force itself into his consciousness. "There's something not right here, Reggie, something very much not right."

# Eleven

Once the peak of the storm had passed, the thunder had wandered off in search of some other innocent dog to frighten witless, and the rain had ceased, leaving only the comforting dripping sounds of wet trees, Sanford gave Reggie a handful of his favourite kibble in reward for keeping him company and being such a good listener, and led Reggie back to his luxurious, dry kennel.

The night was not a restful one for Sanford. Fragments of thoughts crept in and out of his mind under cover of a fitful sleep. Images flickered behind his closed eyelids, too fleeting and too out of focus to capture. There seemed to be recurring and surreal unsettling strobe flashes of a man falling into a hole, of a car falling through space, of a woman crying.

As happens in dreams, time often seems not to matter or not to play any sort of recognizable role, and in this dream the scene and the action changed abruptly but in a way that the dreamer found entirely acceptable. New images appeared. They were images from Sanford's recent past, and he knew this in the dreamlike way best described as "just somehow". The images shifted and tumbled, and although they were not unpleasant, they made him feel increasingly uneasy. One image began to stand out.

The image became clearer, more appealing, more evocative. A young face hovered above his. Curly blond hair hung down. She smiled, then giggled.

"Hi Daddy!" More giggling.

"I sent you something." And then joyous laughter.

"I hope you come home soon", but then an impatient voice sounded from an indeterminate direction in the middle distance.

"Julia!"

The child's smile collapsed, then slowly began to form again. "I have to go now. Mommy's not well again."

"Julia!"

The image shimmered, began to dissolve. Sanford reached out in panic, trying to touch the face, the hair, the beautiful blue eyes, but he grasped only at air, darkness began to fall, and then Sanford realized that he was reaching up into the night, sheet and blanket thrust off his chest which was now covered in sweat.

He recognized the features of Joe's bedroom, having their cloak of invisibility lifted by the first grey fingers of dawn.

Sanford uttered a single rough expletive, climbed out of bed, got himself a glass of water, then returned to bed hoping to sleep for another hour or two.

Twenty minutes later, it was clear that all possibility of sleep was gone, and Sanford climbed again out of bed into the thin light. While washing, shaving, and dressing, he tried to put in place a plan for the day. There was still material in Joe's office to go through, but there was also some thinking, pondering, to be done. He decided to spend an hour or so weeding Joe's vegetable garden and having a morning romp with Reggie.

Reggie was lying casually in the doorway of his largish kennel, one paw crossed over the other, one half-opened eye scanning the world in front of him, but his head rose in greeting as Sanford approached, and his tail thumped one wall of his kennel. Sanford had only to feign an energetic jump to one side, and Reggie was out and running, ready for his preprandial exercise. They both galloped around like puppies, Reggie's sudden energy and his delighted barking being enough to dispel any grey mood. After fifteen minutes of that, Sanford put down a generous breakfast for Reggie, and then spent an hour and a half weeding. Not having looked closely at the garden in a couple of days, he realized that some harvesting would soon be in order, and began planning how to use the fresh vegetables that he was already listing in his head.

While weeding, he was able to approach the topic that seemed to be behind his dream just before awakening. The child was his daughter, his beautiful Julia. The voice was that of his ex-wife, Helen. She had been "ex" now for almost six months. Two months ago, one of Helen's friends, someone who was also sympathetic to Sanford, had approached him and made an impassioned plea for him to try to get together again with Helen. Sanford heard her out, but then walked calmly through all the reasons why it would not work, and concluded by saying, "Believe me, I have looked at this six ways to Sunday, and if there was even a glimmer of hope I would leap at it. But it simply will not work."

That much had become obvious to Sanford during the approach to divorce court, and the divorce arrangement itself. The evidence of Helen's multiple adulterous affairs was so clear and so unambiguous that no judge could ignore it. Nevertheless, the two of them, Helen and Sanford, were encouraged to go through counselling and mediation. The only thing that accomplished, from Sanford's point of view, was to show that Helen was deeply in denial about something. The counsellor took him aside near the end of their counselling sessions and said that she thought Helen ought to see a therapist.

"A therapist? That will be a faint hope, I'm afraid. Why do you think she would benefit from a therapist?"

"There seems to be something that is well beyond what we might accomplish through counselling."

"What is it?" Sanford asked.

The counsellor was reluctant to go further.

Sanford gave her a direct, focused look. "Tell me what you think. You can't just raise something like this, then refuse to give your reasons."

"Please be clear that I'm neither a psychiatrist nor a psychologist. But I have seen a lot of couples. I'm afraid that your wife might be suffering from a borderline personality disorder, and I really think that she should see a therapist. Therapy might be able to help her."

"Is that what might be driving her self-destructive interest in sex?"

"It could be part of the reason. Or not. I'm not a therapist, but if you can influence her at all to see one, I strongly recommend that you do that."

Sanford looked at her for a moment. "You've seen her and heard what she's been saying, and probably you can get just as good an idea as me on what she's thinking, perhaps even a better idea. I'll try, but I think things have gone too far for her to take any notice of my suggestions, especially something that might be as incendiary as recommending therapy."

Sanford made the effort, and opened a discussion with Helen. It went nowhere, ending volcanically in less than half an hour.

"Therapy!" she had shrieked in the end. "Whose fucking idea was that? Yours? I'm not crazy, I just made some mistakes, the kind of mistakes that people make all the time. It's me who's paying for that in blood, not you! And now you suggest therapy on top of everything else? You can just fuck off! You hear me? Fuck off!"

Despite the emotional wounds that Helen's actions caused, deep and painful wounds, she was still exquisitely attractive to Sanford. The sandy hair falling over her shoulders in long graceful waves, the arresting pale grey eyes, the perfect nose, the mouth that curled up slightly more on the left side than on the right when she smiled, and the smooth unblemished skin, these were the things that had smitten him in biblical might the first time he saw her, and he was attracted by them still, in all their visceral power. He recognized that this was partly just pure physical allure, but also partly the residue of the deep love he had once had for Helen. However, love for an image, a phantom, a memory, is a dead end, a road terminating in a brick wall. It took him weeks to admit finally that there was neither a way back nor a way forward with Helen. It was the end. The long, drawn-out, wrenching discussions he had had with Helen, now tearful, now screaming, now wanting to start over, now defiant, these were signs of an insuperable barrier. When he finally admitted to himself that it was over, that he really would have to let her go for good, he was overwhelmed by an unspeakable feeling of bleakness. The finality of it all, the bitterness of this personal defeat, at having to walk away from the person he had felt was his life partner, turned him into a psychological wreck. He came out of that situation slowly, through the help of a few solid friends, and by burying himself in his job, both of which allowed time, the great healer, to do its work.

The court case had been brief, as these things go, and turned out just about the way his lawyer had predicted. Divorce granted on grounds of adultery. Custody of the daughter given to the mother. Father granted visiting rights one week out of two. His lawyer, a sympathetic-looking woman in her mid-thirties, had forewarned him not to expect custody, but had also said that the settlement would be far less onerous than most, in the financial sense, and that his primary ongoing responsibility would be to provide support for his daughter, Julia.

A deep voice interrupted his flashback. After a few seconds, feeling that he was still being ignored, Reggie gave another low "woof".

Sanford realized, in some puzzlement, that he was standing in front of the compost pile, soil and bits of weed still clinging to his hands. Brushing his hands together over the compost heap, he turned to Reggie, who was sitting in front of his kennel, as though reminding Sanford that there was unfinished business still to transact.

"What would I do without you Reggie?"

Walking toward the kennel, he stopped so that dog and man were facing each other, as though each was looking for answers to unasked questions.

"Two years ago, things could hardly have been better. I had a perfect soulmate who shared everything with me, a beautiful daughter who was the centre of our lives, a loving mother who had become a close friend, and a one-in-a-million mentor and friend I had known since before I could walk. Now, my wife is an ex, and a screaming virago beyond any hope of reaching, my daughter shuttles back and forth and I know that she doesn't understand and isn't happy, and both my mother and my lifelong mentor have died. What I have left is you, Reggie. Tell me what I should do."

Reggie gave another low "woof".

"Get back to Joe's office and get to work, is that it?"

The tail wagged hesitantly.

"That's what I thought you'd say. But I know you're right, so thanks."

The tail wagged more decisively.

"Tell you what, Reggie. It's a little early to be thinking about this, but I've just decided I'll make myself a mushroom risotto tonight. How would you like to join me again on the porch?"

Sanford reached down to ruffle the fur on Reggie's head, and the dog gave his hand a couple of gentle licks.

Because of Sanford's time spent with the vegetable garden and Reggie, the world now looked a somewhat better place than it did an hour earlier.

Back in Joe's office, Sanford was able to immerse himself in the files with new energy. He had thought of digging once again straight into the remaining files that Joe had labelled "Personal", but he decided instead to complete some of the actions that he would take to dedicate a portion of Joe's financial resources. He made a list of the various end uses that seemed the best way to commit some of Joe's estate. Once he began, this work took on a momentum of its own, and before he knew it, early afternoon had rolled around. But he now had some quite definite plans, tasks to gain approval for those plans, and a list of the people he wanted to talk to about his ideas.

At three o'clock, he rose from Joe's chair, stretched, and decided to take a long walk through the meadow and poplar forest behind Joe's barn. He found and pulled on long hiking pants that were gathered at the ankles, good hiking boots, and at the last minute decided to take his camera as well. Despite the fact that it would mean an hour combing the burrs and tangles from Reggie's fur, he decided to take Reggie as company.

Having committed to a number of positive steps as part of his review of Joe's files, he was feeling much better, more buoyant. It took Reggie less than a second to realize that the two of them were going for a walk, and he began bounding about and yipping in anticipation. Sanford locked up and the two of them struck out.

Despite the fact that the sun had poured energy onto the landscape all morning, the grass was still damp from the previous night's storm. Sanford's pants and boots were waterproof, so he didn't mind squidging through the odd wet patch of ground. Reggie abandoned whatever concerns he might have had, and was soon a sodden mess, carrying a large cargo of burrs, grass seeds, twigs, mud, and anything else that could hitch a ride. The meadow was huge, about 600 metres wide and more than a kilometre long, and it was a meadow because the soil here was only about twenty centimetres deep, above a layer of mixed rock and subsoil, lying on limestone bedrock about a metre down. The centre of the field was a sea of daisies, and Sanford wandered toward them, recalling similar rambles in his past. The buttercups of his youth smiled up at him once again. He found morels and false morels. He remembered suddenly that on the east side of the meadow, not far from the stream, was a large patch of wild strawberries. Their season would be finished now, but he moved in that direction anyhow, soon coming across the first of the lovely, delicate little strawberry plants, and seeing them extend almost to the bank of the stream.

Skirting the edge of the strawberry patch, he came to the stream and then turned north. The stream was in good flow from the previous day's storm. Birds were singing in the poplars on the other side of the stream, Reggie was galloping everywhere at once, it seemed, stopping every few minutes to take a ritual drink of water. At the north end of the meadow, still several hundred metres distant, was the edge of a pine forest, where the white pines grew in clumps, neighbouring clumps being separated by about ten or so metres of sparse grass. The two of them, man and dog, wandered into the pines, and were immediately engulfed by the quiet and peace that these large trees commanded. The trees swayed and whispered. The needles underfoot yielded to Sanford's step and made no sound. The air wafted scents of terpenes, some light and volatile, others as heavy and resinous as the sticky pine gum that was so hard to remove from hands and clothes, and that made you think twice about climbing a pine tree.

Sanford and Reggie wandered for about half an hour through the pines, Sanford saying nothing, Reggie rushing about, snuffling, and uttering an authoritative bark at the odd squirrel or chipmunk. In a large clearing, a flat rock, covered in cool moss, presented an inviting seat, which Sanford accepted. Reggie was circling energetically to one side, literally following his nose.

"Reggie! Time to go home!"

Sanford struck out, knowing that Reggie would always be aware of where he was, and headed to the west before turning south into what he knew was a large stand of juniper. The sun, the wind, the pine pollen, the scents rising to meet him from the grasses and flowers, these had the same effects on him that he remembered as a youth, banishing worries or concerns, burnishing a positive view of the world, and above all giving an immense feeling of peace. They entered the stand of juniper, Reggie off somewhere to the right, not trying to be quiet or subtle at all. The air here was filled by a much richer odour, more monoterpenes, having that intoxicating camphor-like scent typical of junipers.

The juniper stand yielded to a strip of grassland, which then led straight into the arc of pines within which rested his and Joe's great stone table.

"We're home, Reggie! Come on! Time to clean you up!"

Reggie bounded past Sanford, ears flopping in the way that probably reflects a dog's view of heaven, and galloped round the end of the house toward his kennel. When Sanford reached him, he had slobbered a drink from his bowl, throwing water everywhere, and sat panting in blissful exhaustion.

Apart from being a mess, he had three porcupine quills sticking from the fur around his nose.

"Okay, Reggie. Let me get the scissors, and we'll take those out."

Reggie gave a suppressed yelp as each one came free. There was then the rough hand-combing, to get out the worst of the twigs, mud, and grass, following which Sanford settled down to the job of dislodging all the remaining woodland hitchhikers Reggie had picked up over the past hour and a half. It took almost twenty minutes of combing and brushing, but when they were finished, Reggie's coat shone and Sanford had four large clumps of dog fur, mixed with meadow and forest debris.

"How about a spell on the porch, Reggie?" and within five minutes Sanford, now in shorts and a T-shirt, and Reggie, still sporting his canine dinner jacket, were relaxing over lemonade and kibble, respectively. Sanford checked his watch: five fifteen. There was still work to do on Joe's files, but the afternoon was almost gone, and there was no good reason to break the glow that surrounded the two of them.

Life was good.

The rest of the afternoon and early evening drifted by – the preparation of Sanford's risotto, its slow consumption, once again on the porch in Reggie's company, and then three hours spent rereading parts of Marshall Berman.

Closing his book, Sanford resolved that tomorrow he would dig into the remaining files in Joe's "Personal" compartment. A glass of Balvenie knocked away the last of the chocks, and the good ship Sanford glided effortlessly down the slipway into a deep sleep.

# Twelve

In the middle of the night, Sanford's cellphone rang.

It was July 8, six days after Joe's death.

"Hello", Sanford mumbled blearily into the device. "Hello."

"Hello. James Sanford?"

"Yes, this is Jim Sanford. Who, who am I speaking to?"

"Mr. Sanford, this is Sergeant William Howell at Metro Police. I will come straight to the point, Mr. Sanford. There's been an accident."

Sanford struggled to peer through the fog bank that filled his head. "Wait a moment. Wait a moment. Why isn't someone here in person to tell me this? And how do I know you're with the police?"

"Yes, I'm sorry Mr. Sanford, but we thought it best to get the information to you as soon as we could." He then gave Sanford his shield number, asked him to call Metro Police 52 Division, ask for Inspector Meloni, and have Meloni confirm the call. This operation took Sanford about three minutes, then Howell came back on the line.

"It's your wife, Mr. Sanford."

"You mean my ex-wife."

"Sorry sir. I wasn't sure."

"What about Helen?"

"I'm afraid she has died in St. Michael's Hospital, a little more than half an hour ago."

"Died? How? What happened? How did you get my number?"

"Your address and telephone number were in a notebook in her jacket. Are you in Toronto, sir?"

"No. I'm in Stanley Falls."

There was a delay at Howell's end.

"Near Peterborough", Sanford added.

"Can you come to Toronto right away, sir?"

"Yes I can", but then Sanford suddenly panicked. "Julia! My daughter! What about Julia? Is Julia all right?"

"Yes sir, she is all right. A police officer and a social worker are with her at your wife's condo. She's fine, sir. Can you come to Toronto? I can meet you wherever you like."

"Er, yes. I will come. Meet me in the lobby of my condo building", and Sanford gave the sergeant the address.

"I'm leaving now", Sanford said and put the phone down. His hands were shaking. Looking at the clock, he understood the reason everything was dark: it was quarter to three in the morning.

Sanford threw on some clothes, pocketed his cellphone, made sure he had his wallet and keys, grabbed the small notepad from its spot by the phone in the kitchen, where he had jotted down local numbers, and raced out to his car. The unexpected wrenching news about Helen had once more raised spectres, and Sanford had to work hard to keep the black thing under the manure pile from rising up before him in a ghastly victory dance.

There was no traffic on the roads, and the trip to the city was the fastest he had ever done. If there happened to be some eager young buck out there with a radar, well, tough. His travel time to the condo was a good three quarters of an hour shorter than anything he had previously clocked. He parked in his spot in the garage of his condo building and took the elevator to the lobby. A large police officer was standing, hands behind his back, next to the window just inside the main door.

"Sergeant Howell?" Sanford demanded rather brusquely, checking the shield number on the officer's cap.

"Yes, sir. Mr. Sanford."

"I want to see my daughter right away. You can explain to me what happened on the way there."

Howell nodded, and they walked quickly outside to his cruiser.

There was still very little traffic about, Howell drove quickly but competently, and without needing his siren, and they stopped in the turning circle in front of Helen's building. During the short ten-minute trip, Howell described in brief but neutral terms what had happened. She was found in a park, barely alive. She looked like she had dressed in a rush. Some items of her clothing were found in a handbag that was lying next to her. Howell said that she had been rushed to hospital, but…

"Who found her?" Sanford asked.

"It was a night owl walking his dog."

Howell said that they didn't have more details than that at the moment.

Images of Helen flashed before him, and the knowledge of all he had lost with her struck him again like a body blow. Sanford realized then just how deeply he still had loved Helen, even after all the betrayals, after all the screaming and acrimony.

"How much does my daughter know?" Sanford asked suddenly.

"Nothing. Unless the social worker has told her a bit over the past couple of hours. I expect they would have sedated her. I understand that she was asleep when the building administration staff let us into your wife's – ex-wife's – condo."

"Was my daughter alone?"

"I believe so. Yes, sir."

The elevator doors opened, and they walked the short distance to the door to Helen's condo.

The place was in chaos. The sink was piled in dirty dishes. Clothes were scattered over the floor, and it looked as though nobody had cleaned any surface in weeks. A police officer sat on a cleared half of the couch and was working or making notes on a tablet. She stood as Sanford and Howell entered. She introduced herself as Constable Douglas, and before Sanford could utter the question clamouring to be asked, she assured him that Julia was fine. The social worker had given her a mild sleeping tablet and was with her now in the bedroom.

The bedroom was in no better shape than the rest of the condo. Used tissues and open containers of makeup littered the table of the small, cheap vanity set. The clothes hamper had dirty blouses, skirts, T-shirts, and undergarments spilling from it, and a small pile of obviously soiled clothes lay in the corner next to it. The clothes closet was open, clothes hung askew from hangers, and some had dropped to the floor.

The sheets and pillows were grey.

The social worker sat quietly in a chair next to the bed. In the bed, Julia lay sleeping in the innocence of youth, her blond locks spread in charming confusion over the pillow. The social worker, whose ID tag said she was J. Bennett, was probably in her late thirties, and in a face that looked very tired, two bright blue, solicitous, deeply sympathetic eyes met Sanford's. She rose, put a finger to her lips as a shushing signal, and led Sanford quietly out of the room.

"She's fine. I'm guessing you are Mr. Sanford. She awoke when we arrived, and she was confused but not upset. We thought it best not to tell her anything, and I gave her a sleeping pill almost immediately. She knows nothing."

The rest of the condo was just as much a shambles. The bathroom was disgusting. The spare room, which was where Julia normally slept, was neat, but the covers on the bed were turned down, and the bed looked as though it had been slept in.

"Did you wake her up, here in this room, when you arrived?" Sanford asked the social worker, and apologized immediately because it had come out sounding like an accusation.

"No. We found her in the bed where she is now. It looks as though she left her own bed and went into her mother's room."

And her fucking mother wasn't there, Sanford said accusingly to himself, and immediately regretted the thought. Helen had been ill.

Helen's few visits to doctors had led nowhere, possibly because she was not forthcoming, possibly because the health system was too obtuse either to see there was a problem or to do anything about it. Helen fairly obviously was in denial, at least it seemed obvious to Sanford. He could not convince her to get help. And now this had happened. He raged inwardly against himself and the entire world.

Fuck! Fuck! Fuck!

Sanford made an effort to calm down. He looked around the condo slowly, hoping that his examination would be interpreted by the social worker as a critical review that yielded a "Fail" verdict.

"This place is a mess", Sanford began, keeping his voice as matter-of-fact as he could. "How could you have let my daughter continue living in – this?" and he swept his arm around indicating the whole sorry jumble. "Why didn't somebody contact me?"

The social worker's reply bore the signs of professional patience and human exhaustion. "The condo is indeed a mess, Mr. Sanford, but it's not unhealthy. It's not infested by anything. There's plenty of good food in the fridge. Your daughter is clean, she shows no signs of being undernourished, and there are certainly no signs of abuse. We can't take away someone's children just because they're bad housekeepers."

Her reply was so measured, and so full of sympathy, that Sanford's incipient anger was deflated right away. She was right. The important focus now was the future, however unsavoury the past might have been.

"How long will she sleep?" he asked.

"Probably only three or four hours more. She should awaken at about eight o'clock."

"When she's awake, I want to take her out of this, this chaos, and to my condo. We can have breakfast there together. I assume there will be some paperwork…"

"Yes. I have it here. All you need to do is sign. We can have a more formal meeting later to fill in all the details. I just need two pieces of identification from you, Mr. Sanford."

These minor formalities took no time, then it was finished.

"I'll stay around until she's awake", the social worker offered.

"You don't need to, thanks. You probably have other work to do."

"I have home visits to make, but I can't start those for another three hours at least."

Sanford looked around once more. "Are all the places you visit as bad as this?"

Bennett smiled weakly. "I only wish they were this good."

As though waking from a light sleep, Sanford said in sudden resolve, "I'm going to tidy up a bit."

He began in the sitting room, collecting newspapers and magazines and piling them onto an end table, then picked up all the dirty clothes, found a large black plastic bag under the sink, filled it and placed it in a hall closet. From the same closet, he drew out a broom and pan and gave the living and dining room floors a quick sweep. Finally, he spent half an hour washing the mountain of dishes that covered every surface in the kitchen and filled the sink to overflowing. Bennett quickly laid down her leather documents case and helped. When that was finished, Sanford found a small suitcase in a closet, and packed as many of Julia's clean clothes as he could find. He also packed her small teddy bear, Abner.

Sergeant Howell returned at that point, just finishing a call on his cellphone.

"There is something we can do, Mr. Sanford, if you feel up to it."

Sanford gave him a quizzical look but said nothing.

"We can go to the condo where we think your ex-wife was prior to being found in the park. There might be some things of hers there and if so we would like to keep them separate from everything else in the condo."

Sanford nodded mechanically.

Howell drove them to the condo, which was in a new building on Adelaide Street. On the seventh floor, Howell broke the police seal on the door to unit 712, and pulled on latex gloves.

"How did you know that Helen had been here?" Sanford asked.

"One of our technical support guys noticed a cellphone number on the business cards that were in her handbag, and asked to have a look at the cellphone. When we found it wasn't in her handbag, we used GPS to trace it here. It was found behind the sofa. Must have slipped down there at some point."

Howell let them into the condo.

"Don't touch anything sir. We can walk through the unit room by room. Let me know if you see anything you think might belong to your ex-wife."

The condo obviously was home to a single man. The walls were painted in strong colours of battleship grey and matte rust, the furniture was no-nonsense tinted glass, stainless steel, and leather. The dominant colours of the furnishings were black and rust. A high-end sound system and a flat-screen television dominated the living area, the floor was expensive parquet and there wasn't a carpet in sight, the few pieces of art were hard-edged abstract or austere black, white, and grey prints of street scenes, winter trees, and one of a demolition site at dawn.

The bedroom was large and had an impressive view to the south. The bed was unmade. Howell opened the closet door, Sanford peered in and shook his head. There was nothing in the bathroom or kitchen that caught his attention.

"There's nothing of hers here that I recognize, Sergeant."

"Very good, sir. We can leave now." And he began entering something into his cellphone.

Sanford hesitated. He took one long last look around the large living-dining room. The artwork. The contrasting maroon and steel-grey walls. The brands of the sound equipment and TV. The three pictures that sat together on top of what looked like a sideboard. Howell was still busy with his cellphone and Sanford took advantage of Howell's distraction. It took only a second for Sanford to capture the image using his cellphone.

"Okay. Let's get out of here, Sergeant."

As they walked back to the police cruiser, Sanford asked, "What did she die of?"

"It looks as though she was strangled, but we'll know more when all the evidence has been examined."

"What other evidence is there?" Sanford asked.

"I shouldn't be saying this sir, but since her cellphone was found in that apartment we need to check for any physical evidence that she was also there."

"What kind of phys –" Sanford began, then remembered the bed.

They had reached the car. Howell held the door for Sanford.

"I can't say anything more, sir", he said.

Howell took Sanford back to Helen's condo via the morgue, where he identified Helen's body. It took him fifteen minutes to stop shaking.

The next two days were a trying time.

He called Anne Ferguson, explained what had happened, felt his gratitude for her as her sharp intake of breath sounded over the telephone, and asked if she would see that Reggie was fed and looked after. She said yes, of course, she would do that, expressed her shock and sympathy through a voice that was already beginning to crack up, and made sure that she had Sanford's cell number.

He called his boss and explained what had happened.

"Oh, my God, Jim! Oh, my God!"

Long pause.

"Okay! You're off work for a month. Look after your daughter. Sort things out. Don't worry about work." There was another pause here. "And if you want to talk, Jim, call me any time."

Sanford spoke to Helen's parents, who had already been informed and were devastated, but even so their first concern was for Julia.

Then there were the details that had emerged on Helen's death.

The police had determined that she had been in the apartment where her cellphone was found. They had found evidence that she had been in the bed there. Based on that evidence, the police said that a couple of theories were being pursued, but wouldn't elaborate beyond that. They said there would be more details after the post-mortem results were released. Sanford wanted to know absolutely everything, but at the same time he absolutely didn't want to know anything.

Inspector Meloni had summarized what he could for Sanford. It wasn't much. Sanford stood there, a hundred questions fighting for priority in his head. Meloni evidently sensed his inner turmoil, and put a friendly hand on Sanford's shoulder.

"Your ex-wife is dead, sir. We appreciate your assistance thus far, and I don't expect we will have any follow-up questions, although it's possible. Try to forget about all this. I know that's a stupid suggestion, but I think it's the best advice I can give. Look after your daughter. She needs you. Leave the rest to us."

Helen's funeral took place four days after her death. It was not a large gathering: Helen's parents, a dozen friends, Anne Ferguson, Stephen Maxwell, Sergeant Howell, Inspector Meloni, and Ms. Bennett. Sanford chose not to say anything, either during the short service or at the graveside. But he did throw three roses onto the coffin once it was lowered, and then he began to break down.

There was a tug at his sleeve.

"It's all right, Daddy. Mommy is happy now."

Said in matter-of-factness and all sincerity. *Out of the mouths...*

I really do hope so, Sanford thought. I really do hope so.

They left the cemetery at about one o'clock. Sanford declined, with thanks, several requests to "come back to our place". He and Julia drove to Sanford's condo. The first thing they did was change into summer clothes, shorts and short-sleeved tops.

"Would you like to go for a walk?" Sanford asked, and Julia's face brightened in response as she nodded yes. They spent two hours walking along the boardwalk on Ward's Island talking about everything and nothing, stopped for ice cream, stopped again for chips, stopped a third time for soft drinks and watched the sailboats drift past on the lake. The summer sun shone onto Julia's face, making her even more radiant than usual. She was a child goddess. The breeze caught her hair and flipped it whimsically around her shoulders.

Back at Sanford's condo, he and Julia made a cake for dessert, and cooked spaghetti and meat sauce, which they ate listening to Julia's favourite music, Peter Ustinov's "Peter and the Wolf".

It was clear, even before they had finished dinner, that the stress of the past days and weeks was bearing down heavily on Julia. She was dog-tired, and Sanford carried her few things to the spare room, made up the single bed for her, laid on top of the sheets the flowery quilted bedspread that he had retained after his divorce from Helen, plugged a pale night light into the socket to one side of the door, and helped Julia change into her pyjamas. Her eyelids drooped, and she was as limp as a shot rabbit, but she smiled as one arm repeatedly missed the armhole of her pyjama top. Once she was tucked in, Sanford began reading "Peter and the Wolf" to Julia doing his best imitation of Ustinov. He barely made it to the end of the first page. Looking down at her placid face, taking in the delicate, intoxicating scent of little girl, he thought of the rhyme "Wynken, Blynken, and Nod" that he used to recite to her, and realized that he and Julia had a lot of catching up to do, a lot of ground to cover; the little girl would very soon become someone altogether different. As a last thought, he laid Abner, the teddy bear, on the pillow next to her head.

Apart from making best use of every second with Julia, Sanford had chosen to have no plan at this point but to take it a day at a time for a little while. He sat at his computer, did a quick and successful search, then leaned back and realized that a more definite long-term plan for his time with Julia already was forming in his mind, of its own volition, and based on wisdom that he recognized instantly.

At a deeper level, another, very different plan was also emerging.

# Thirteen

In spite of the previous day's strains, Sanford slept well, waking just before six.

Within a second, his mind leapt to Julia who presumably was still asleep in the next room. Rising and peering into her room, he confirmed this, smiled at the sight of her and Abner, her teddy bear, cuddling in sleep, and returned to his own room to dress. Recalling Julia's typical breakfasts, he went to check that he had everything needed for them to begin the day. Overnight his mind must have been solidly at work, because a list of all the things that needed doing, both short- and long-term, scrolled through his thoughts.

Today, however, was not the time to be slave to a plan. Sanford thought of several activities that they could undertake, and they would decide together which one should take priority. It was going to be another warm, sunny day; he busied himself on tasks in preparation for breakfast, but all the while his mind dwelled lovingly, and at length, on how he and Julia would spend their time.

"Daddy?" Sanford must have spent more time daydreaming than he realized. Julia came slowly along the hallway, her pyjama top and bottom askew, wiping the night from her eyes, and yawning.

"Hello sweetie", he said. He walked toward her, picked her up, and brushed strands of hair from her face. "Did you sleep okay?"

"Mmmm", she murmured, nodding.

"How about some breakfast? After you wash and get into some fresh clothes."

"Can I have toast and jam?"

"Yes, toast and jam for two, I think. Do you want help washing and dressing?"

"No Daddy", she said in mild reproach. "I can do that myself."

It took her surprisingly little time to re-emerge from the bathroom, and she was well turned out for the day. She was wearing pink shorts and a plain white cotton top, but what impressed Sanford most was how neatly parted and brushed her hair was. The thought occurred to him immediately that she probably had had to learn a number of things fairly quickly herself, that her mother couldn't be relied on to do the mother-daughter things that other mothers would reserve jealously for themselves. It was an uncharitable thought, especially coming so soon after Helen's funeral, but it took up an immediate and stubborn residence in his mind.

"Let's have breakfast outside, on the terrace", Sanford suggested. "You bring the napkins and the jam."

The terrace was large, about 200 square feet, it faced southeast, and was a principal reason for Sanford choosing this particular condo. The gentle power of a new day flooded in from the east. Five floors below, the city had already rumbled to life, the fresh morning breeze wafted enticing aromas from Sanford's herb garden, and in their boxes, fastened to the terrace walls, a gossip of petunias nodded together, and whispered their plans for the new day. A rustic picnic table occupied the central portion of the terrace. The napkins were held in place against the morning breeze by the jar of raspberry jam, and soon plates of toast, spoons, knives, and large tumblers of juice gave the table an air of breakfast in the great outdoors.

Julia had two thick slices of toast, unusual for her as far as Sanford could remember, and she looked up regularly to smile across at him. Despite recent events, he had not felt this relaxed in months.

"I like this jam. The jam Mommy had was never this good."

Sanford was a bit taken aback, looked at the jar, and realized that Helen probably would not spend the money needed to buy Greaves.

"Nothing but the best, Julia", but an inner voice said to him sternly, *You're going to spoil this kid rotten. You know that, don't you Sanford?* He told the inner voice to go screw itself, and was about to ask Julia if she wanted more juice, but she got there first making an unrelated statement.

"I can't find my blue shorts."

"Blue shorts?"

"I have a pair of blue shorts somewhere. Mommy always wanted me to wear pink shorts, but I'm tired of pink shorts."

Sanford couldn't remember packing blue shorts, and Julia took the conversational initiative once again.

"Can we go and buy some blue shorts?"

"Yes, of course. I thought we would drive to Uncle Joe's place today. We can stop on the way and buy some shorts. Would that be okay?"

It was evidently more than okay, because her face lit up immediately.

"Uncle Joe's place! Yes!"

Sanford realized that he would need to explain about Joe, that this wouldn't be easy coming so soon after Helen's death, but his instinctive thought was to invoke the healing power of the country: trees, clouds, open skies, birds, sunsets, and the inexpressible comfort of being enfolded by quiet rural nights.

Once a trip to "Uncle" Joe's had lodged itself in Julia's mind, all else was crowded out, including, almost, the blue shorts. They carried the breakfast things back into the kitchen, locked the terrace door, washed up, had the requisite post-prandial pee, and packed a small bag for Julia. Sanford ran a hand over his unshaven face but decided that the corrective activity could wait until they were in Stanley Falls. As she climbed into Sanford's car in the condo's parking garage, Julia ran her hand over the upholstery and sniffed the air, and Sanford could easily imagine Julia comparing it to what might have been the chaotic state of the car she had been used to – Helen's car. Sanford was supposed to have Julia for one week out of two, but this rarely worked out right. What had become Helen's disorganized and impromptu approach to life meant that there was practically nothing systematic in what she did. Many times, Sanford contented himself in just having long telephone conversations with Julia, since more scenes and screaming from Helen was something Julia could do without.

After driving for about half an hour, Sanford pulled off the expressway, made his way to a large mall, parked, and they went off in search of the desired blue shorts. Three pairs of shorts later, in different shades of blue, they were back on the expressway, and a bit more than an hour later, Stanley rose.

Sanford drove slowly through the village, and it was clear that Julia both remembered some of what she was seeing, and was excited to be in Stanley Falls once again. He stopped at the small general store, picked up a selection of things that he thought should cover all reasonable whims on what to have for lunch, collected the mail – both Joe's and Aileen's – at the post office, and then drove the last kilometre to Joe's place. They turned into the driveway, and Julia looked around happily.

"Can we see Grandma as well?" she asked.

Anger flared instantly within Sanford, and he did his best not to let any of it show.

*She didn't tell her*, Sanford thought to himself, scarcely believing it could be true. *Helen didn't fucking well tell Julia about my mother.*

It was bad enough that he had received a confused telephone message from Helen saying that she and Julia would be in Montreal and couldn't make it to Grandma's funeral. Dodging the need to see Sanford again? Flipped out on another of her binges? Who knew. But not telling Julia at all about her grandmother was unforgiveable.

"Let's get our things inside first. And we have to say hello to Reggie."

"Yes!" Julia said in sudden anticipation. "Reggie! Can we see Reggie right away?"

"Okay", Sanford agreed through a lopsided smile. "Let's go say hello to Reggie."

Reggie had heard the car arrive and he was standing next to his kennel, waiting. Julia ran around the house to the back, Sanford walking quickly to keep up with her.

"Reggie!" she cried when she saw the dog standing there. Reggie's tail rose and began wagging weakly in greeting, but Sanford got the definite impression that the dog was really thinking to himself *Oh Christ! Here we go again!* But soon they were both running around the backyard, Julia laughing and Reggie barking happily, until she threw her arms around the dog's neck and they rolled in the grass like old friends.

After a few minutes of this, Sanford clapped his hands and said "Okay. Enough roughhousing with Reggie. Time to get our things inside."

The next two hours were sombre, and Julia shed tears of shock and grief at hearing that Uncle Joe had died, and then also that Grandma had died. They talked for almost two hours, Julia breaking into tears every half-hour or so.

"Did you tell Mommy about Grandma?"

"Yes, I did."

"Why didn't she tell me?"

"I don't know Julia. But Mommy was not well."

And there the discussion ground firmly onto the rocks.

"We should have a little something for lunch", Sanford said after a longish pause.

"I'm not very hungry."

"I know, but we shouldn't skip lunch. How about a small grilled cheese sandwich?"

"Well, okay, but just a little."

By the time Joe's kitchen was filled by the tang of grilled cheese, Sanford knew that "just a little" would be nowhere near enough. They both chowed down on generous sandwiches, and in Julia's case this included enough ketchup to drown a small cat. Cold water from Joe's well, which was one of Julia's pleasures at Joe's place, washed down their lunch. As Sanford expected, it took only twenty minutes or so for Julia's eyelids to begin drooping, and he led her off to one of the places she most liked to nap, the big sofa in Joe's library. She was out almost instantly.

There was nothing urgent among Joe's items of mail; a few of the letters required a response, and Sanford would do that later that night once Julia had gone to bed. The same was true of Aileen's mail items. Almost.

One letter was from a Toronto legal firm, evidently the result of discussions with Cartwright at the bank. It requested that arrangements be made for the handover of a safe deposit box that was being held in trust by the Toronto firm and was to be transferred to Sanford on Aileen's death. Sanford had no idea what this meant. A quick call to Cartwright confirmed that he was aware of this; he agreed that it was an unconventional, even odd, arrangement, but despite that it was all above board. Cartwright promised to set up an appointment for Sanford with the Toronto firm for 10 am the following Wednesday.

Sanford was taking a bit of a chance here, since he intended to drive to Toronto early that morning for the appointment and drive back the same afternoon, leaving Julia in Anne Ferguson's care for the day. Anne had never met Julia, but was dying to do so, and Sanford expected they would get along just fine.

The visit to the legal firm in Toronto would wrap up the last loose end from Aileen's will. One of the things coming out of dealing with his mother's estate was Sanford's becoming aware of the fund that had been providing Aileen her modest income over many years. This was a fund that had been set up by her husband, Harold. Aileen had always said he was a first-rate salesman and that during all the time she knew him, he was always winning awards for best sales record of the month, quarter, year, and so on. These awards were often substantial monetary prizes, and Sanford assumed that it had been this money Harold had used to set up the fund he had established for Aileen. One of the things Sanford had realized only quite recently was that Harold had left Aileen just three years after they had been married. But even during those three years Harold had been home probably less than six months in total, the rest of the time purportedly being spent on the road, selling. Sanford didn't buy it at all, but he had so little respect for Harold that he had no interest in pursuing whatever the truth might have been.

Working his way through the remaining papers linked to Joe's will was a bigger job, and after making the arrangement via Cartwright, Sanford turned to that task. He managed to spend a little more than half an hour at it.

"Daddy? Can we go and watch the river?"

"Oh, hello Julia. Yes, of course we can. Did you sleep all right?"

"Yes. I like Uncle Joe's books. It feels almost like he's still here."

"Watching the river" meant sitting on the dam, listening to the deep-throated roar as water flowed over the multiple weirs in thick curved slabs, watching the sea of bubbles this produced just below the dam, feeling the occasional eddy of mist brush their faces, cool and damp. But "watching the river" also meant then walking to the bakery, buying a butter tart each, strolling to the dock next to the bridge, and eating the tarts while dangling their bare feet in the water.

"Why is everybody dying, Daddy?"

"Well, not everybody is dying. Uncle Joe and Grandma were getting old. And Mommy died because of an accident. We've just been a bit unlucky the last little while, you and I."

"You're not going to die, are you Daddy?"

Sanford smiled despite himself. "No Julia", he said, putting his arm around her and giving her a strong hug. "You and I are going to be spending a lot more time together, and that's a good thing. We have a lot to do, stuff we haven't been able to do until now, good stuff, and some new stuff. Don't you worry about today, or tomorrow, or next month."

One of the items at the back of Sanford's mind, but occupying him more and more, was Julia starting school. He had been surprised and alarmed to find that she had not been going to kindergarten, something that Helen had said was happening. Where Julia should attend school was another open question, and one that had to be decided soon.

Their butter tarts finished, they stood up, flapped their feet around to dry them off, pulled on socks and shoes, and began walking back to Joe's place.

"When we get back, we'll take Reggie out for a proper walk."

"Okay."

"And we'll do some weeding in Uncle Joe's garden."

"Hmm."

"And we'll go to the bank so I can get some money. You're an expensive young lady to have around."

"No-oo!" she said through a giggle. "But okay."

"Then we'll meet Mrs. Ferguson."

Here there was a nod.

"Then we'll take a drive to get some special food for Reggie."

"Yes! Reggie!"

"Then we'll sit down and think about what to do for the rest of the summer."

"Okay."

There were plenty of things that Sanford wanted to do with Julia, and he had already begun writing a list in his head.

# Fourteen

It was summer.

The days shimmered and billowed in an effortless and seamless continuum that reflected the remembrance of youthful summers, at once insubstantial and all-consuming, dreamlike but also firmly anchored in time and place. Sanford's time revolved around Julia, and slowly formed a rich pastiche of images and sensations: breezes kissing bare skin and ruffling hair, wild flowers in meadows, fingers black from gardening, romping with Reggie, reading books in the evenings, cooking dinners on the barbecue, having long lunches in the sylvan glade, and Julia making pies, muffins, cakes, and cookies with Anne Ferguson.

Julia relaxed noticeably. She and Sanford still had discussions every few days about Helen, as Julia tried to deal with her great loss, but also with the confusions and disappointments she felt during her time alone with her mother, and Sanford tried to nudge Julia toward a kindly view. Both Sanford and Julia had made it a point to talk every week to Helen's parents, who were having great difficulty coming to terms with what had happened and why. They had undertaken grief counselling and that seemed to be making a difference. And certainly their regular talks with Julia, while a sad reminder of their daughter's terrible end, had the net effect of being a great tonic for them. Sanford recognized some features of both himself and Helen in Julia, but he saw also that there was emerging, even in her childhood, a distinct and independent individual who was aware, inquisitive, intelligent, and in a strangely mature way eager to grab life in both hands.

Sanford checked in with his boss every four or five days, not because there was anything Sanford needed to do, but because Maxwell was concerned, anxious for better news, news of healing that he hoped would be forthcoming, and playing the role of a solid professional friend. Sanford had a rough idea when he would return to work, but the one time he mentioned it to Maxwell had brought a strong response warning Sanford off that kind of talk. "Let the situation evolve", he said. "You and your daughter have had a large disruption and new ties will take time to form", he said. "Don't fuss over coming back to work", he said, "not even on a casual basis".

But while Julia's world relaxed, mellowed, and glowed in a kind of new-found happiness, Sanford's world was developing a dark side. There was a relaxed togetherness, there was laughter, and there emerged aspects of their growing daughter-father bond that sometimes took Sanford's breath away. But there were encroaching clouds, subliminal, below the horizon, more ominous for being all but invisible.

Sanford's meeting with the Toronto legal firm went off as planned. His time away from the various urban veneers, interfaces that had been a central feature of his professional life, now made these trappings strike him as slightly comical and immodestly overblown. Was this the fantasy world that he recalled Joe speaking of more than once? Was Sanford having some of Joe's success at merging the healthy unsophistication of the country and the unhealthy sophistication of the city? The bank draft that was being handed to Sanford on Aileen's death came as a considerable surprise: a little more than $250,000 capital that had been managed in order to deliver to Aileen a regular

$15,000 a year, while trying to keep the capital sum constant. Could this much money have come just from bonuses and money that Harold had saved? And why would Harold do this? Guilt? Had Sanford judged Harold unfairly? He had no idea, but the incentive to find out just was not there. At least there was no doubt as to where some of that money would go: an education fund for Julia.

The legal aspects of Joe's will had been sorted out now, and the necessary paperwork all completed. What remained were the literary and personal aspects Joe had left in Sanford's care. Sanford continued to work away at the literary material in odd hours, he had now assembled a volume of Joe's poetry that would probably extend to about 180 pages, and that collection was almost ready to go to a professional editor for a first assessment. To Sanford, Joe's work was brilliant, and raised images in his mind that were as clear and arresting as those Joe's reading programme had provoked in the youthful Sanford decades ago. He was midway in the job of working through Joe's essays, and these were every bit as exceptional as his poetry. But there was probably another thirty hours' work to be done on that before he could even think about seeking a second opinion. And even his work on Joe's essays was something Sanford undertook ambivalently, considering himself hardly in Joe's league, but committed to the task by the last wishes of his best friend. Beyond all that, there still was work to do on Joe's "Personal" material, but the surprises uncovered thus far gave Sanford pause, and the thought of dealing with the remaining material caused him some trepidation.

Julia soon made friends with three girls her age in the village, and while this changed her outlook a little, she seemed still to be most at home secluded with Sanford at King Arthur's Rectangular Table. Sanford thought he could see, hoped that he was seeing, the same magical fascination, the same multi-level awakening in Julia that he had experienced in his own youth. Joe's spirit floated above and around the place, but would that be enough? Would there be inspired in Julia the things Sanford had known as a child and as a youth? The urge to an unending refinement of subtlety, sensuality, connection to nature? A recognition of the delicate but irresistible power that beckoned from within the indefinite depths of the sylvan glade? The promise of both peace and complexity? Watching his daughter closely, Sanford was gravitating more and more toward having Julia enter school in Stanley Falls rather than in Toronto. It was clear that Julia felt some atavistic ties to Joe's place, whereas there really were no connections for her in Toronto. Sanford would dearly have loved to know just what activities Julia had while she was under Helen's care, but the only time he had raised this with Julia, she clearly didn't want to talk or think about it, and the shutters closed firmly.

Sanford had taken to inviting Anne Ferguson over to Joe's house once or twice a week for an evening meal, and it was clear to Sanford from the first of these occasions that Anne and Julia had fallen into a comfortable surrogate mother-daughter friendship. Anne revealed an educated palate, not only for food but also for wine, and the three of them had some rare evenings, Julia taking part oenologically by means of watered-down wine. At the third of these occasions, Anne proposed, and Julia and Sanford agreed readily, that they have a corn, hamburger, and sausage roast.

This was so much a summer activity, so reminiscent for Sanford of unending sun and warm breezes, tree canopies saturated in birdsong, days having no schedules or deadlines, the bounty of high summer, and in general time's thread unwound recklessly, luxuriantly, from its spool, that he threw himself into the project with gusto. Julia soon caught the gusto bug, and the three of them started developing lists of food and drink, and the people to be invited. They decided quickly enough to keep it small, since large parties create worries and organizational hassles that steal the very fun those parties are intended to generate, and they settled on a list of fourteen people, including the families of Julia's three new friends. These people were all known to Anne, who soon rolled up her metaphorical management sleeves and took control of invitations. Several telephone calls indicated that the coming Saturday, two days hence, would be perfect. All schedules were clear and the weather promised to be summer-perfect. Sanford was assigned the role of chief provisioner, and Julia would give her rubber-stamp final approval to all the arrangements. There were earnest discussions about how big the hamburgers should be, how many hamburgers per person they should prepare, what kind of sausages they should buy, and at the last minute Julia suggested that they also barbecue chicken pieces. They discussed where all this would be eaten, where people would sit, how the corn would be cooked, how Reggie should take part, and then Anne said that they couldn't have just meat and bread, and she and Julia began to plan a monster potato salad. There was some good-natured arguing, a lot of laughing, and both Sanford and Anne twinkled to see that Julia had become almost unbearably excited. Sanford went off to buy the meat, soft drinks, wine, napkins, paper plates, cups, potatoes, onions, and various other bits and pieces, sending over his shoulder an unbroken string of narrative on where to get the best local corn, that he would commission the sausages specially, and that Joe's recipe for hamburg patties was a killer. He was still talking to the other two as he climbed into the car, and just then he needed no reminder that although recent losses were still fresh, their sharpness was receding and his life very quickly seemed to be turning toward more pleasant scenes.

He came out of the local general store bearing four large shopping bags, and a promise that the chicken pieces and sausage would be ready by the next day. Less than an hour later, he shook hands with Leslie Baxter, an old farmer whose farm had slowly transformed itself into one of the more successful market gardens in the area, and loaded five large bags of freshly picked ears of corn into the car. The entire exercise left him almost reeling under the flood of memories, surging up from his own youth, of hay, fresh tomatoes, peas in the pod, cucumbers, and a range of fruits and berries. Deciding to collect Joe's, Aileen's, and his own mail on the way back through the village, he bounded from the car into the post office, a newly acquired lilt animating his step, tossed the few items of mail onto the passenger seat, except for one addressed to him, which he opened right away, and then was hammered right back to Stone-Age oblivion by its contents.

# Fifteen

Not able…

Not able to have…

Anderson, Howard, and Blanchard…

*Dear Mr. Sanford,*

*Attached is correspondence recently brought to our attention by our banking partner, and related to our letter to you on July 3 concerning the monies transferred to you on instructions from Mr. Harold Sanford. This correspondence should have been included in the documentation we sent previously concerning the transferring of funds to you, but this was not done due to an oversight which the Bank acknowledges. On our own account, and on behalf of the Bank, I hope you will accept our sincere apologies. Please contact the undersigned should you have…*

Not able to…

Sanford had read through the two-page attachment quickly.

Not…

Now he read it again, more deliberately.

Was this some kind of sick joke?

He let the letter fall onto his lap and gazed vacantly out the car windshield. He had an image before him of fabric unravelling, a sense of the ground falling away from beneath his feet, and no handholds to grasp.

Not able…

Everything was confusion. It wasn't real. It couldn't be.

Pulling out his cellphone, Sanford dialled the number on the letterhead.

"Anderson Howard and Blanchard", said the clipped professional voice of the receptionist.

"Albert Blanchard, please."

"One moment, please."

Short delay.

"Blanchard."

"Mr. Blanchard, this is James Sanford speaking. I've just received the letter you sent me. I have a couple of questions."

"Certainly, Mr. Sanford, but if we will be getting into details, I suggest you come to our offices." As Blanchard spoke there was a shuffling of paper in the background.

"No need. This is straightforward. First, I want to confirm, to be absolutely sure, that the letter I'm holding is genuine. Did you send me a letter dated July 13 that begins 'Attached is correspondence recently brought to our attention'?"

There was the sound of pages being turned, and more shuffling of papers at the other end. After a short delay, Blanchard said "Yes, Mr. Sanford, I confirm that."

"And are you sure that there is no doubt about the authenticity of the attachment and the veracity of its content?"

"There is no doubt, sir. Something having this sort of implication we have double-checked and triple-checked."

"Thank you, Mr. Blanchard. That's all for now."

"You're welcome, Mr. Sanford", and the connection was broken.

Not able to have ch...

Sanford looked over the attachment again, more closely. It was dated July 5, about three weeks after Aileen's death.

> *Dear Mr. Sanford,*
>
> *At one time you knew me as your father, although I am not. I loved Aileen dearly, but I have always been morally weak. My weeks and months on the road as a salesman were extremely successful commercially, but they put me in the way of temptations that I was powerless to resist. Worst of all, however, I abandoned Aileen when it became evident that she was not able to have children. Money is a cold means for trying to amend being absent and unfaithful, but it's all I have to give. I tried to provide adequate support to Aileen while she was alive. Please do what you will with the money being transferred to you now that she is gone.*

Sanford's old anger for Harold surged again, this time in seemingly implacable power. There was also hatred, and confusion, and loathing, and a desire for revenge, and...

Suddenly, Joe was beside him. "Calm down Jim. Work it out."

"Easy for you to say!" Sanford shouted, and a woman passing looked at him suddenly and dubiously through the half-open passenger side window.

Sanford started the car and drove straight back to Joe's place. Leaving the groceries in the car, he quickly entered the house, sat down at Joe's desk, and began a conversation with Joe.

"What the fuck's going on, Joe?"

"Why did it take all this time for me to find out? This is pretty fucking significant information, Joe."

"Who am I, Joe? My mother was not my mother, and I have no idea who my father was. Who am I?"

There was a long pause here.

"Joe. You must have known something about this, Joe. All those years, Joe. If you did know, and I can't believe that you didn't, why the hell didn't you say something?"

One of Joe's frequently repeated statements came to Sanford: "Things are not always what they seem, Jim."

"Shit, Joe! I don't need your folk wisdom! Not now!"

But Joe's calm voice was still there. "Work it out, Jim. The reasons people do things are complicated."

Sanford sat there a while longer, stewing, but, to his own surprise, calming down just as Joe would have had him do.

Almost as though Joe had prodded him, Sanford realized he was in a present that included other people who mattered to him and who depended on him, that he simply had to swallow all this and get back into the nuts and bolts of everyday stuff, into the excitement of the corn and burger roast. Throwing any sort of damper over that event was simply not on the cards. He forced himself to smile, even if it felt fake and hollow. Neither Julia nor Anne could suspect that anything was wrong, that any major shift had occurred for him.

Fiercely suppressing the emotional confusion that roiled within him, Sanford rose decisively, went out through the back kitchen to a small shed behind the house, and retrieved the wagon that Joe had always used to drag grain to the barn and bring in vegetables harvested from the garden. Sanford loaded the wagon high in the bags he had collected during the past couple of hours, dragged it all triumphantly across to the home where he had spent his childhood, which he now cursed viciously and unfairly as being parentless, and forced a broad grin in response to Julia's squeals of delight, and Anne's smiling applause.

For another half-hour the three of them sealed pairs of corn ears into plastic bags to prevent the corn drying out, stowed the onions and potatoes in storage bins, placed the wrapped hamburger meat in plastic containers ready to be carried over to Joe's large fridge, checked that the barbecue out behind the house was big enough to churn out food at the appropriate rate for fourteen people, confirmed that there was enough charcoal, and began imagining where seating would go, where they would put the condiments station, when they would get the ice and where the soft drinks and wine would be laid out, how many waste containers they would need, and how to prevent napkins from blowing all around the garden.

Having done all they could that day, Sanford and Anne laid out plans for a day of preparations the next day, Friday. Anne and Julia would spend much of the day making potato salad, and discussing all the things that go along with preparing food but have nothing to do with food.

Julia and Sanford dragged the wagon home, unloaded the few remaining items from the car, hauled them to the back of the house, and stored them in the back kitchen.

"Can we have chicken tonight, Daddy?"

"Funny you should ask", Sanford said. "I was thinking of some nice chicken in barbecue sauce", and the response indicated that that would be more than adequate.

They prepared and cooked the meal together: chicken smeared in barbecue sauce and baked in the oven, some rainbow noodles, and fresh peas.

"Can I try some more wine tonight, Daddy?"

"Would a nice Chardonnay be all right?"

"Yes, that would be fine", his budding taster announced in confident sophistication, even though as far as she was concerned "Chardonnay" could have been the name of a company that made trailer hitches.

Less than half an hour after finishing their companionable meal and doing the washing up, the small half glass of wine and the day's excitement did their thing.

"I'm tired, Daddy", and she was nodding off even before she finished pulling on her pyjamas.

Sanford sat by her bed for a few minutes, then rose quietly, went into Joe's den, and closed the door. It was going to be a very long night.

# Sixteen

Sanford was living through something unique in his experience: not having a provenance, not having a complete past, not knowing where he came from, not knowing just how he got here, or why, not knowing who he was. Or maybe the unease really came from a complementary negative: knowing for certain that he didn't know any of these things.

Not only was it unique, it was unsettling. Dizzying. A visit to the edge of a personal abyss. Disorienting. And it brought out a previously unknown sensation: a powerful aversion to being rootless.

The initial shock was past now, but even as he sat there, he experienced aftershocks, as his mind travelled over the same ground again and again, following some urge for self-inflicted wounds, like the urge to pick the scab that had formed a few days after the previous scab-picking exercise. At an intellectual level, he was aware that an abrupt change had occurred in what he had considered an unquestioned and stable past, and that he had to come to terms with this. He was also aware of an overwhelming uncertainty that had invaded his existence like a tsunami.

It was pointless to deny or try to rationalize away the urge to know who he was. He had to know. But he couldn't allow it to turn into an obsession. Dogs and cats have no idea where they come from, but you don't find them frozen into a state of existential panic. No. They are generally happy, given loving owners. They play. They purr. They wag tails and bark in invitation. They roll on their backs. Their lots in life are good, and they just accept all this at face value.

But people aren't dogs and cats. They can't avoid thinking. They have a need to know things, especially things essential to a sense of who they are.

So. Sanford was raised by someone who turned out not to have borne him. It wasn't possible for her to have been unaware she was not his mother, so she must have known how he came into her care. Why didn't she tell him? These lines of thought raised other questions about the why, how, where, and when of Aileen. She had reasonable schooling for someone raised in her time, and she had used this to do secretarial and bookkeeping work for various people in Stanley Falls and nearby towns and villages. Her family came from this region, but she was an only daughter, and her parents had both died while they were still relatively young. Was there any good reason why she stayed in this area? She could have done better in Kingston or Peterborough, or even in Belleville, or Cobourg. Why stay in a deep rural hamlet? Did any of this have something to do with her silence?

Joe probably knew as much about Sanford's background as anyone, and possibly quite a bit more given his acute analytical capabilities. He stayed in Stanley Falls for very definite reasons, one of which was that he had inherited his property, and it was indeed a gorgeous place for him to become rooted. Judging from the literary drafts Sanford had seen, his farm sat well with his artistic impulses, and gave them fuel and free rein as well. Joe had been a combination older brother, uncle, and close friend to Sanford. Had he done this out of other-than-normal interest, concern, and affection for a young boy who had no father figure in his life? Had Joe taken any other youth under his wing in the same way? Not as far as Sanford was aware. Apart from whatever he saw as his role with respect to Sanford, Joe must have had considerable knowledge of Sanford's past, and probably knew that Aileen was not his biological mother. It was fair enough that he would say nothing if all he had were suspicions, but if he had definite knowledge, was there a good reason why he would not eventually tell Sanford?

Before drifting off into realms of nested speculation, Sanford needed to go through, once again and more carefully, all the "Personal" files Joe had left to his care. If Joe had not told him important things while Joe was still alive, it was entirely possible that he would have left an account, or at least hints, for Sanford to read after Joe's death. But this seemed sneaky, underhanded, and completely unlike Joe.

Sanford began digging into the files. They formed a stack about eight inches deep. It would take at least five hours. He began making notes on a fresh pad of lined paper. The approach he decided on was to make two passes: the first to note down anything that seemed to him to be of particular importance, and the second to record in detail anything that would help fill in the picture of his life, formulate any questions that this material suggested, and try to find answers to these questions.

At 11 pm, Sanford had completed his first pass, and had already made five pages of jottings. He had uncovered few answers, and there were now many more questions. He rose from the desk, stretched, and went to check on Julia. She was out for the count, but it looked almost as though a little smile of amusement remained on her lips.

At 3 am, Sanford stopped again. He rose from the chair, stretched, and this time went outside. The cool night air was fresh, still, and silent. The rich, resinous odour of pines and other evergreens pervaded the night, and Sanford stepped down from the porch and walked to the back of Joe's house. Reggie had emerged from his kennel and was standing to greet Sanford. Sanford fussed him for a good five minutes. Reggie occasionally cocked his ears at something Sanford was unable to hear, but it seemed clear that the local rabbits had learned, probably from the gruesome public failures of one or two of their number, that attempts to get past Reggie and into the fenced-off garden were simply not worth it. The low roar of the river at the dam in Stanley Falls was just audible, but the rest, the peace of Joe's little demesne, and the quiet of the area it was set in, filled Sanford's spirit. Just then, he felt very close indeed to Joe in one sense, but held apart from him by the disappointment, the frustration, and, indeed, the anger stirred up by all the unanswered questions that now swirled in Sanford's head.

Back at Joe's desk, Sanford applied himself once more to the files. He was in the home stretch now. By 4:30, he had completed a close reading of all the material. By 5:30, he had done all he could, but had found few new hard facts and had drawn few conclusions. The primary hard fact was what lay beneath Joe's manure pile, and the moment he recognized this, images from that day returned, trailing their ominous wake. The significant conclusion was that there was just one person remaining he had to consult. There was no indication he would learn anything new from that person, but he had to try. Having read all Joe's notes thoroughly, some of the questions he had were now clearer, some of Joe's life, at least those parts that he felt sure he knew reasonably well, made a little more sense. There seemed to be more rationale for some of Joe's actions. But still, too much of what he once thought he knew about Joe was now shrouded in uncertainty. And it had been that shift from past certainty to present doubt that had given him the most trouble. At least, however, the night's work had made his next step clear.

Having completed a good deal of online searching, he decided when he would have a talk alone with Anne Ferguson. He emailed his boss and asked his agreement to a new schedule that Sanford proposed.

And, most significantly, he did one more thing. That one thing would provide what he hoped would be a change of scene, a break, a means at the very least for he and Julia to get away from the trouble and angst that life had thrown at them both over the past few months, and, maybe, take the first steps in a new start. It would also allow him to check the last potential source of information, to take the only remaining step that could allow him to close the book on what his many years with his friend Joe had meant.

He booked flights for himself and Julia to Milan, and connecting flights to Genoa, and at 6:30, he switched off his computer.

# Seventeen

Sanford was sitting pondering many unanswered questions, trying to decide which ones were "right now urgent" and which could be set aside for the time being.

"Daddy?"

"Hello Julia. Did you sleep well?"

"Yes." A delay here while she appeared to be thinking about something. "Could we have breakfast outside?"

"Yes."

"At the big stone table?"

"Yes."

"With Reggie?"

"Yes. What would you like for breakfast?"

"Can we have pancakes?"

"Would you like plain pancakes, or blueberry pancakes…"

"Blueberry!"

Of course, Sanford had suspected that as soon as the blueberry option came up, everything else would take a back seat.

"Why don't you go and wash and get dressed, and I'll see you in the kitchen in a few minutes?"

"Okay." But she remained where she was.

"Daddy?"

"Yes."

"I love you. I wish Mommy was here too, but I love you and that's enough." And she then turned decisively and left the room.

After the series of jolts Sanford had received during the past week, that was just about the best medicine he could hope for, and he felt weak and strong at the same time.

Sanford busied himself laying out the ingredients for pancakes. He was about to begin preparing the batter when Julia came back, dressed in a pair of her new blue shorts. The two of them had a nice smiling discussion about shorts and new clothes and then Sanford said they should give Reggie his breakfast before they had theirs, so they both trooped outside to where Reggie was waiting as though he had heard and understood everything they had said during the past few minutes. Julia hugged Reggie, and her eyes-closed smile said everything about carefree youth and being fully in the moment. Reggie put up with it all dogfully as part of the assumed cost of finding the shortest path to some grub. They watched Reggie eat for a while, then went back inside, washed their hands, whipped up the pancake batter, and then did the pancake road test.

For quite a few years, Sanford had mused, at odd and idle moments, about whether there was something fundamentally significant, some inherent primeval element of hilarity and magic that was triggered in young minds by the sight of a pancake turning end over end in the air and landing back in a skillet. Sanford had recognized Julia's attraction to this culinary sideshow when she was not yet two, and he had acquired the skill of flipping a pancake so that it sailed straight upward to within a few inches of the ceiling, then fell reliably back into the pan. The road test complete, and the giggling having subsided, the serious task of frying thick spongy pancakes, heavily laden in blueberries, began. Carrying plates of pancakes, a jar of maple syrup, cutlery, napkins, and a damp cloth, they moved out toward the sylvan glade. A call to Reggie from Julia brought the dog bounding around the corner of the house, since Reggie had always been keen to join Joe and Sanford at the stone table.

They sat there, all three of them, since Reggie was allowed to sit on the stone bench next to Sanford. Julia had a cushion to raise her up enough so that she could lean over her plate and avoid dripping syrup on her clean white top and new shorts. They ate wordlessly, Sanford giving a small piece of pancake to Reggie every few minutes.

When they had finished, they both made good use of several napkins, and then Julia looked at Sanford and giggled.

"What?" he asked, through a half-smile. "Oh! I bet it's my teeth."

"Are mine black too, Daddy?"

"Black? Julia dear, your mouth looks like an oil well."

"Can I show Anne?"

"No, we'll go and brush our teeth when we take the dishes back to the house. If Anne saw you like this she'd probably faint."

Having returned the dishes to the kitchen and washed them, they went to brush their teeth, but Julia broke into paroxysms of laughter when she saw herself in the bathroom mirror. After that had died down, they brushed together, then went back to the kitchen.

"What are we doing today, Daddy?"

"Well, there are quite a few things to do for the corn and sausage spectacular tomorrow. We can prepare the hamburg patties this morning. That will probably take about two hours. Then I think we should go talk to Anne. But right now we need to talk about a holiday."

"Holiday?"

"Yes. In a little more than a week, we will go to Toronto, we'll stay at my place, and we'll spend some time visiting Grandma and Grandpa."

"Why is that a holiday?"

"Oh, no. That's not the holiday. The holiday comes right after that. I thought we would go away for about two weeks."

"Go away? Where?"

"Someplace you've never been. To Italy. Do you think you'd like that?"

"Would I be with you, Daddy?"

"Yes, certainly. It would hardly be a holiday otherwise, would it?"

"Then I think I would like that. Will we eat some spaghetti?"

"We'll eat lots of things you haven't eaten before."

"Oh! Yes, I will like that!"

"Well! You're becoming a real foodie, aren't you?"

"Foodie?"

"Yes. Somebody who goes crazy about food."

"But isn't that everyone, Daddy?"

"Yes, I guess it is."

Sanford wiped down Joe's large food preparation area.

"Okay. Let's get out the hamburg meat, leave it to warm up, then we can make the patties. How many hamburgers do you think we'll need?"

"I don't know."

"Well, how many hamburgers would you be able to eat yourself?"

"Six."

"Six! That's a lot of food. And don't forget, there'll be corn and sausages and chicken and potato salad and then dessert."

"Oh! Yes! Then maybe just two."

"Okay. Fourteen people and two hamburgers each, that's twenty-eight hamburgers, so let's say thirty-five hamburgers altogether just to be safe."

Sanford pulled two large plastic containers of hamburg meat from the fridge and set them on trivets to warm.

"While the meat is warming, what do you say we go over to Anne's place and see what plans she has for today? I'm sure she's going to need your help."

# Eighteen

Sanford accompanied Julia across to Anne's place, she was given a generous motherly welcome, and Sanford explained that they had begun preparations for the big picnic. Anne clearly had vast plans of her own in that area. She whisked Julia away, and soon they were deep in cosmic culinary discussions that clearly excluded Sanford just by their nature. Sanford took that opportunity to duck out and deal with some loose ends. Back at Joe's place, he began making his calls.

"Inspector Meloni please", Sanford said, then waited for the clicking and buzzing to finish.

"Meloni."

"Hello Inspector. This is James Sanford. I wanted to follow up on a few details on my ex-wife's death."

"Yes sir. There might be only a limited amount I can tell you."

Sanford ignored this caution.

"I would like a copy of the post-mortem on Helen. Can you help with that?"

"Yes sir. That report has been issued and I can send you a copy."

"Good. Thank you Inspector. Now. Can you tell me where you are with the case?"

"No sir. I can't discuss that with you."

"So the case is still open?"

"The investigation is ongoing."

"And my ex-wife's belongings, have they been released yet?"

"They're available to be picked up. It has to be her next of kin, either her father or mother."

"They've both been hit very hard by this", Sanford said, rather pointedly. "They're also both elderly and not that mobile. I assume that one of them has to sign for Helen's effects?"

Meloni indicated that yes, that was the case.

"I can bring my father-in-law in and help him through the process. Does it take long?"

"No. We need only some identification and a signature."

"What's the procedure, where should we turn up?"

Meloni gave Sanford the details and the location, and said that he could turn up any time between eight in the morning and six in the evening.

Sanford then called his in-laws, Gillian and Philip. Both of them had been close to Helen, and it was difficult to say which of them was having the greatest difficulty coming to terms with what had occurred. Sanford had only to substitute himself for Philip, and Julia for Helen, and he understood clearly the yawning chasm they had to face again every morning and endure all day every day.

"Hello?"

It was Philip. His voice was listless, drained of life.

"Hello Philip. This is Jim. I hope you are both doing well."

There was a silence. "As well as can be expected, Jim. I guess. How is Julia?"

"Julia is fine, Philip." It had occurred to Sanford to say something like "Young people roll with problems more easily than adults", but there would be no purpose in that. Sanford actually did suspect that because Julia could not avoid seeing the way her mother had lived every day, could not avoid seeing the decline, she had to come to terms with the very large changes in Helen's behaviour compared to what she had known just months earlier, and that she was in fact in a better position to handle the ultimate loss. But who knows how these things can affect children, and what impacts they might have later?

"We've decided to have a corn and sausage roast. It's to take place here tomorrow, and Julia is up to her elbows in the preparations." On a whim, Sanford extended the offer for them to come. "I could easily come into town, pick you up, and take you back on Sunday. We have more than enough beds here."

"Very kind Jim. But I think we'll have to decline. I doubt very much that Gillian would be up to something like that, and I have to say that Philip is also firing on fewer than all cylinders."

They talked about things in general before Sanford broached the difficult matter he really had called about.

"I guess we do have to collect her things", Philip said slowly, and the pain that came across the phone to Sanford almost broke his heart. Sanford suggested what he had in mind, and Philip agreed reluctantly.

"Very well then, Philip. I'll see you on Monday morning about eight o'clock."

"Won't you have to leave very early for that?"

"I always rise early anyway, Philip. It's no inconvenience for me. And the earlier we arrive at the police station, the less likelihood there is that we'll be stuck behind a large gang of people."

Philip agreed, the arrangements were made, Sanford asked if there was anything he could bring them, to which the answer was "No thank you", and they ended the call.

After he had hung up, Sanford sat a long time, thinking about things. Sanford had come to terms with the situation. Sort of. At least that's what he told himself, but there was more than a little truth to this. Each of the events in the long series that ultimately resulted in the seismic shattering of his once-loving relationship with Helen had taken its turn in converting the tenderness they knew first to individual wounds, then to generalized flayed agony, and ultimately to protective armour. The armour was a calcined shell covering his emotions. Even now, unless Sanford was vigilant, individual scenes could be activated and replay themselves inside his head. Helen's repeated and flagrant betrayals, the many discussions that Sanford had tried to initiate with her but that had always resulted in Helen exploding into very hurtful screaming matches. Then there was the slow formal torture of the divorce process, even though it was short-lived, and especially his partial loss and feared permanent loss of Julia. Those demons were all still lying in wait. Now the sad and sordid tragedy of Helen's long decline had descended into a police investigation.

Sanford shook his head. This was familiar ground, and what the hell could be the point in tilling it yet again? Somehow, there had to be a line drawn beneath it all so that he and Julia truly could head off in a new direction.

But where to draw the line? Good question. In trying to separate out, segregate, permanently sequester the corrosive side of Helen's recent persona, how much of Sanford's own life over the past year had to be put under the microscope? But he resolved not to go down that path yet another time.

Sanford turned to the puzzle of his own past, pulled out the notes from the previous night, and began going through them. There was quite a bit of material that had to be digested. And the more he thought about this, the more he was willing to admit that he needed help in getting both the background and the answers he wanted. Sanford opened the notebook containing the list of contacts he had built up during years of work, and picked up his cellphone again.

After half an hour of telephoning, he had three very guarded references to one name: Daniel Conway. The references were guarded, because Sanford had been asking for help in a murky area. He wanted somebody to take a pulse in a particular part of the underworld. These conversations had given him pause, and he sat back to think things through. Exactly what was he looking for?

If Conway took the bait, this would certainly be his first question as well, so he, Sanford, needed to have a clear and satisfactory answer.

Cutting right to the bone, Sanford was pretty sure that he wanted to understand three things.

First, what history is available out there on Harold Sanford? Who is or was he? What has he done, or what do people think that he has done?

Second, what is the current word on Charles Jeffers? Who is he and what does he do? What is his background? What has he been involved in recently?

Third, is there any information or any suspicion of a link between Harold Sanford and Charles Jeffers? If there is such a link, is anything known about the context? Sanford knew that pursuing Jeffers was a dead end, but it wasn't something he could betray any knowledge of, and in any case he wanted to know what people thought about him.

Sanford wrote down these questions, refined the wording somewhat, thought about what any answers might mean for him, and thought about how he would explain his interest when Conway asked, as he would, no doubt.

After staring at his notes for a quarter-hour, Sanford bit the bullet.

"Conway."

"Daniel Conway?"

"Yes."

"My name is Jim Sanford. I would like to talk to you about some information you might be able to get for me."

"Very well. Can you tell me how you got my name and contact information?"

Sanford explained a bit about himself and his background, the contacts he had made over his working life, and the three references he had used to find Conway.

"We will need to meet, Mr. Sanford."

"Fine", Sanford responded. "Tell me where and when."

The arrangements were made, and Sanford was somewhat surprised when the location suggested was the executive bar at a high-end Toronto hotel. They arranged a meet for two thirty the following Monday. This was conveniently on the same day Sanford had agreed to pick up Philip, and take him to retrieve Helen's things from the police. Sanford would have to see if he could make arrangements with Anne to look after Julia for almost the full day. "Cleanup" after the corn and sausage roast would be a done deal by then, or at least mostly so, and he was fairly sure that an offer of help, in the event of unexpected loose ends, would be an acceptable hook to hang this request on.

"Just a few items of information please, Mr. Sanford."

"Certainly."

"Does this have to do with a divorce?"

"No."

"Is a police investigation involved?"

Sanford thought about this for a second. "Yes, but the information I'm looking for has nothing to do with the investigation. As far as I'm aware."

"As far as you're aware. Please understand, Mr. Sanford, that I will not undertake work that could threaten or undermine a police investigation. Please come to our meeting prepared to discuss this in detail."

"I will, and thank you for agreeing to meet". The line had already gone dead.

# Nineteen

On Saturday, the day of the big roast, Julia was out of bed and dressed by six thirty and twanging from excitement. The three of them – Anne, Julia, and Sanford – had developed a schedule, since they were essentially the hosts, and Julia had got fully into the spirit of the thing, even if her lack of practical experience left her dangling, at any one instant, from several incomplete tasks. But all the important items had been completed: all the various meats were prepared and ready to slap on the barbecue, the monster potato salad growled in anticipation from within its huge flowered porcelain dish, the soft drinks and white wine were chilled in Joe's almost commercial-sized back kitchen fridge, the potato chip, peanut, and nacho nibbles were ready to be tipped into bowls, and the various dips were made and waiting to be uncovered. The barbecue had been cleaned, the seating was all arranged, and a large compartmented tray containing utensils, napkins, condiments, and packaged wet wipes was ready to go. They had decided that the corn would be steamed inside Anne's house, rather than barbecued, to help take the barbecue itself off the critical path, and the timing was set for husking the corn and placing it, in batches, into the steaming tray already in place on Anne's stove. Everybody invited had confirmed they were coming.

"All we need to do now is take it easy until we reach the first item on the schedule", Sanford said.

Julia was having trouble with this. Sitting still when there was so much excitement ahead was an area where she lacked practice.

By three o'clock, the first guests began arriving, bang on schedule. Sanford had put two hamburg patties and two sausages on the barbecue just to get the right smells in the air. By then, Julia was struggling to keep up. The potato chips, peanuts, and nachos had been placed on the picnic tables, and people began helping themselves. One of Julia's jobs was to go around checking on when these snacks needed topping up, but she kept being interrupted by her friends and their parents, all of whom wanted her to stop and talk. She was learning the host's role of juggling the tasks of making polite conversation and ensuring that food and drink kept appearing at the right place and the right time. She was rescued from this dilemma by Sanford.

"Okay sweetie, you don't need to worry about the chips and peanuts anymore. We've started laying out the plates of barbecued meat, and people can help themselves from here on."

It was clear that Julia had made the switch from host to participant when one of her new friends came up to her, mouth stuffed full of hamburger, and Julia wandered off with the girl, chattering happily, to find herself something to eat.

Sanford operated the barbecue, and when a consignment of meat was cooked he would carry the tray of it to the central serving table and then spend ten minutes chatting and working his way around the small crowd, before he had to return to the barbecue to look after the next batch. By five o'clock, people were picking at the last bits of chicken and sausage, helping themselves to just a little more potato salad, and exclaiming at how full they were. The gathering was restructuring from amorphous feeding frenzy to small and relaxed social groups. Sanford loaded his plate in hamburger, sausage, chicken, and a generous pile of salad, grabbed two bottles of wine, and wandered around the garden filling glasses and conversing. This carried on for another half-hour, until Anne and Julia emerged victoriously from the kitchen bearing two large single-layer cakes. A communal moan of "I'm too full to eat another bite" along with "but I must try that cake" made it certain that the gathering would carry on until at least seven o'clock on its second wind.

During all the excitement, nobody noticed the nondescript grey Hyundai Sonata that cruised past four times that afternoon.

# Twenty

Sanford turned up at Gillian and Philip's modest but beautifully kept house just after seven thirty on Monday morning. It was a sunny day, and the time and effort Gillian had spent coaxing her garden to do just what she wanted were showing the familiar and spectacular results that Sanford had known and admired for years. Roses and clematis climbed and bloomed elegantly across the front and side of the house. The red and yellow hibiscus that Gillian took in every year to what she called her "winter garden" were as large, blousy, and self-confident as if they were in their native southern states. Beds of annuals and perennials were scattered across the uniform green of the front lawn, bursting in health as usual. Along the winding path leading to the front door, small delicate huddles of pansies, portulacas, and alyssums smiled up at Sanford as he passed them.

Philip answered the door immediately.

"Good morning, Jim. You're prompt as usual."

"Morning, Philip. No point in wasting the day, especially one like today."

Philip looked up at the brilliant blue sky without enthusiasm, seemed like he was about to say something in response, but then just invited Sanford inside.

"Gillian is still sleeping. I don't want to waken her, so could we leave right away?"

"Certainly. Maybe I'll have the chance to say hello to her when I bring you back."

"Yes. Maybe…"

Philip looked like he had aged ten years in a tenth that time. Several years ago, Philip would have been out in the garden in shorts and T-shirt, bronzed from his work at pruning, weeding, and deadheading, and flashing a smile from a leathery tanned face that beamed vibrant health, interest, and engagement. Now, he moved uncertainly, his steps were shorter and showed the anxiety and exaggerated care of the elderly and infirm, his gaze wandered about at random, and his hands seemed to drift through the air, tentatively, indecisively. It was clear that an important bright light had been extinguished from his life, and not for the first time Sanford wished he knew what he might do to ignite another one just as strong.

Philip picked up sunglasses and a rather dashing sun hat. "Shall we go?" he said.

The trip to the police station was not long, and Sanford did manage to prod Philip into talking a bit about his garden, what he was doing in general, what he was reading, and the cooking club he and a dozen neighbours had taken such pleasure in for more than twenty years. A little of the old Philip showed through, but this was pinched off almost instantly when Sanford said "Here we are", as he pulled into the large empty car park as close to the door as he could.

"I don't think I can face seeing Helen's things", Philip said, in a heart-rendingly plaintive tone.

"If you would prefer", Sanford replied, "I'll take her things back to my place and look through them. I have a good idea of what you might like to keep, and I can deal with all the rest. Let's just go in and sign for the things; I'll put them in the trunk, and then I'll take you home again."

Philip nodded without any animation, and almost as if he were acting under duress.

Five minutes later, they were back at the car. Helen's things had all been placed in one large plastic bag, and through the thick plastic's distortions it was hard to make out any individual items. Sanford dropped the bag into the trunk, closed the lid, and drove Philip back to his home.

When they arrived, Gillian was out front watering the flower beds, something that Sanford thought was a healthy sign.

"Hello Jim", she said as he climbed out of his car and went around to see whether Philip needed help. She laid down the hose as they walked toward the house, and asked if Sanford would like a cup of coffee. "We usually have one about this time either in the winter garden or on the patio in the sun."

Sanford said he would love a cup of coffee. They all entered the house, where Philip dropped his sunglasses and hat and led Sanford toward the patio, while Gillian peeled off to the kitchen to make the coffee.

Being offered coffee seemed, to Sanford, a surprisingly social initiative for this grief-stricken couple, and it suddenly occurred to him that the diversion of having someone else to talk to made a difference. It was brought home to Sanford, once more, how much these two people had come to mean to him. He knew that Gillian and Philip were deeply shocked, embarrassed, mortified in fact, at Helen's behaviour over the previous eighteen months, and Sanford was aware that they were relying on him for support. They all knew that Julia played a big role in this, but at an adult level both Gillian and Philip gave the impression of being grateful that Sanford was someone strong they could lean on. As they sipped their coffee, Sanford carried most of the conversational load, which ranged widely, having the apparent effect of relaxing them both, and even drawing out the odd tentative smile. The need to have them come to Stanley Falls, sometime soon, pressed itself on Sanford's mind, and he made a note to get them to agree on dates for a visit as soon as possible.

Eventually, Sanford left, but not before entreating them both to call him any time if they wanted to talk, or just as a change in routine. He reminded them how important they were to both Julia and him, he embraced them both warmly at the door, and Gillian accompanied him as he moved away to his car.

Quietly passing Sanford an envelope, out of Philip's sight, Gillian said "Could you look after this for us Jim? I can't do it and it would be too much for poor Philip."

"Certainly Gillian", Sanford said as he took the envelope. Gillian kissed him, then made her way back to the house. When he had driven a block from his parents-in-law's house, Sanford pulled over to the side of the street, and opened the envelope.

Helen's will.

Her only real asset was her condo, and Sanford realized that it would fall to him to package up Helen's personal things, arrange for the furniture to be picked up and sent to auction, have the condo cleaned and painted, and then make arrangements for it to be put on the market.

Sanford then drove to his own condo and parked in his underground space. He checked his mail, rode to the fifth floor, and spent a few minutes opening windows to air the place. He then got a bucket of water from the kitchen and watered the thirsty flowers ranged around the sides of the terrace. The great volumes of space into which he looked upward and outward from the terrace were saturated in brilliant summer light, and warm zephyrs of mid-morning plucked at his shirt and hair. The sentiment "it's a great day to be alive" presented itself suddenly and firmly in his consciousness, even though the incongruity between this and the pathetic bag of his ex-wife's "effects" could hardly have been greater.

After a long look out over the city, which was bustling and vibrantly alive, Sanford quickly went through the contents of the plastic bag they had retrieved from the police station, found nothing unexpected, decided that most of it would go to a clothes drop box, and then settled in to prepare for the meeting he would have with Conway in a little less than four hours.

The hotel's executive bar was an understated and subdued enclave that spoke of privilege and discretion. It was clear why Conway had chosen it. From any one of the tables, corners, or nooks, all of them complete with massive maroon leather wing chairs, it was impossible to overhear a conversation from even the nearest table in the room. The lighting was sufficiently strong for old, wealthy eyes to read even the finest print. Music played softly enough that it was easily overridden by quiet conversation. Although the space had probably seen tons of Cuban cigars go up in smoke, there was no trace of tobacco staleness in the air.

Sanford was fifteen minutes early, and as he looked around the room none of the five men seated looked back at him expectantly. He chose a seat in a corner three tables from the bar. A waiter came over to him at a measured pace, smiled as would a valued servant who knew his worth, and asked "Sir?"

"Lagavulin, please, sixteen years, and a small beaker of water."

The waiter nodded and turned, assuming correctly from long practice that ice was not needed. Sanford's drink appeared within a minute, was lowered lovingly before him in a heavy authoritative container of cut glass, and placed silently on a thick oxblood leather coaster. The water followed suit.

Sanford hadn't taken his first sip before a man of medium height entered the bar. He had an athletic-looking build clothed in a good navy suit, wore his steel-grey hair short, and had a thin face, dark eyes, a somewhat aquiline nose, and a long, strong chin. He walked straight over to Sanford's table.

"Mr. Sanford?"

"Yes. Daniel Conway?"

"Yes."

Conway took a seat.

They looked each other over wordlessly for fifteen seconds, long enough for the waiter to make a silent reappearance.

"I'll have the same", Conway said, waving at Sanford's glass, before the waiter had uttered a word. The waiter nodded silently and moved away.

"I'm not good at small talk, Mr. Sanford, so please just tell me, in as much detail as you can, what it is you want and why you want it."

Sanford had organized his thoughts and he provided some background, described at length what he wanted to know, and then indicated that all this was something necessary in order for him and his daughter to move forward and reshape their lives. It took him about ten minutes to complete his statement.

Conway didn't take his eyes off Sanford the whole time. When Sanford had finished, Conway nodded after a few seconds silence. "I have some questions."

Conway posed his questions. Sanford answered them. First question. Second question. Third question. Midway through the fourth question, Sanford's cellphone buzzed. He pulled the device from his pocket, looked at Conway, and asked "May I?"

"Please. Go ahead."

Sanford got through "Hello?" and then "Oh hello Anne", but then sat up rigid in his chair and exclaimed "What?!!"

After a pause, Sanford asked "Where is he now?" and then after a further pause he asked "Have you ever used the camera on your cellphone, Anne?"

He nodded. "Okay. Please take two or three pictures of his face. Yes, right now."

Another delay. "Good. Now, have you ever sent pictures to anyone using your cellphone? No? Okay, here's how to do that", and Sanford explained the process. "Please send the pictures to me right now, wait until I confirm that I've received them, then hang up and call the local police right away."

By now, Sanford had begun to shake visibly. He looked at his phone, pressed several keys and icons, then said "Okay Anne, I have them. Now call the police immediately."

Sanford put his phone away and rose. "I'm sorry Mr. Conway, I have to leave. Someone just tried to abduct my daughter."

Sanford was hurriedly starting out on what would be a sprint to his condo followed by a high-speed run to Stanley Falls, when Conway said "I will do this work for you, Mr. Sanford."

Sanford recognized the speed at which Conway's mind worked from the question he asked as Sanford was reaching into his pocket.

"Can you forward to me the pictures you were just sent?"

Sanford and Conway dropped onto the table forty dollars and a business card respectively, Sanford scooped up the card and ran from the bar.

# Twenty-one

Sanford's race back to Stanley Falls was close to the record he had set a few days earlier when he had sped the other way after receiving Sergeant Howell's early morning telephone call. By some miracle, he didn't catch the attention of any of the expressway speed patrols. His overheated car screeched to a halt in the drive of Anne's house. He rushed inside and was met by Anne and Julia calmly having glasses of fruit juice.

"Hello Jim", Anne said past a faint smile, but her hard stare at him clicked right away. Julia didn't really know what was going on, and Anne wanted to keep it that way.

"Hi Daddy."

"Hi sweetie." There was a pause here. "Could I have a glass of juice, please?"

Anne relaxed, and Julia smiled, went to the cupboard, found a glass, and poured Sanford a full measure. He sat down as calmly as he was able.

"So", Sanford began, "did we get everything cleaned up from the roast?"

"Yes Daddy. We had seven cooked pieces of corn left, and Anne and I took the corn off and made it all creamy. We had four cooked sausages left, and Anne and I had them for breakfast. We had twelve pieces of chicken left, and Anne said we could make them into Chicken Catch a Tory for dinner. We had some cake for lunch. Would you like some?"

"Well, yes, that would be very nice, since I didn't have much lunch." Within a few minutes, a large square of lemon cake appeared before Sanford, and he ate it with gusto, making I'm-really-enjoying-this noises.

Sanford was relieved that Julia was happy, her outlook unclouded, and very relieved that she was still there and in one piece, and he struggled mightily to behave for the remaining hour before dinner as though nothing out of the ordinary had happened.

At five thirty, Anne began pulling things from her fridge. "I think you both should get washed for dinner. It would be nice to eat outside under the apple trees. Off you go then."

And they did have a pleasant dinner under the trees, although bits of things sporting strange shapes and colours seemed to keep dropping onto Sanford's plate, to Julia's great amusement. Julia talked about a number of projects that Anne had evidently suggested to her, and Sanford, a faint smile fixed on his face, sat back, listened calmly, and tried to suppress the turmoil that was raging deep within him. In due course, they finished, Anne collected plates and cutlery and carried them into the house, and suggested that they all move to the sitting room where they could flop in plush chairs. Within twenty minutes, Julia began to nod sleepily.

"Okay dear", Anne said. "Off to bed with you and have a little nap", and Julia allowed herself to be led away without complaint or resistance.

Ten minutes later, Anne was back. Her expression was now one of concern, and she spoke softly in response to Sanford's curt demand "Tell me exactly what happened".

"It was about one thirty or two o'clock. Julia and I had finished the last of the cleanup and there was a knock at the door. The man at the door, the one I sent you the photographs of, smiled when I answered. He said that you had asked him to escort Julia to Toronto for a short stay with her grandparents. I said I was surprised at that, that I didn't think Jim worked that way, and that he could leave, and I closed the door as firmly as I could. But he stopped it closing altogether, I had my foot against the bottom of the door, but then he just burst in. Julia was in the room she uses, and I found out later that she was listening to her iPod, so she was unaware of any of this. Well, the door opened with such force that I was thrown back against the stove and counter, and he began barging in. But then Reggie hurled himself onto the man, who was caught completely off guard. They both fell and rolled on the floor, and then the man stopped moving."

"Stopped moving?" Sanford asked in puzzlement. "Why?"

"Because I hit him with my biggest skillet. It made a satisfactory clang."

She smiled at the memory, but then her chin began quivering, and she broke down. "Oh Jim, it was horrible. He was a horrible man, and then I thought I had killed him, and then when I realized that I hadn't killed him I wished that I had, and I almost struck him again."

Sanford rose and comforted her. "Anne, you are an absolute brick, and I can't thank you enough. Could you tell me what happened after that?"

She dabbed at her eyes using a cotton hankie she had pulled from a pocket, and described how she had tied the man up using butcher cord, how she had called Sanford and then taken and sent the pictures, and how she called the local police who arrived less than five minutes later. When they found that the man had no identification and was carrying a small gun, they dragged him off straight away. Another local police officer had come to her house by then, and he sat with her and took a statement.

"They said they want to talk to you as soon as possible."

Sanford nodded. "Will you be okay here while I go down to the police detachment? I'm not sure how long it will take."

"Yes", she said, now in a stronger voice. Sanford reassured her he would be back as soon as he could.

As he was getting out of his car at the cop shop, Sanford's cellphone buzzed. It was a text message from Conway.

> *Identity of man whose pictures you forwarded. He is Arthur Wakelin. Minor villain for general hire. Surprised he was used for this job. Obviously your neighbour was seriously underestimated. Still digging. Conway.*

Inside the detachment, Sanford eventually met a Sergeant Nokes, someone he didn't know. Nokes explained that the suspect was being grilled as they spoke, but that they had got little out of him thus far and did not know his identity. The car he had used was registered to someone else from Toronto, and that information had been passed on to Metro Police accompanied by a request for information on the car's owner.

"What will you do with him?"

"Well, so far he's up for possession of an illegal firearm, entering, and assault, and maybe possession of stolen property, depending on what Metro says about the status of the car. He'll probably be transferred to Peterborough to a holding cell. Beyond that, I can't say."

"Do you know if he was here for the day, or has he been staying somewhere locally?" Sanford inquired.

"I can't really say, sir. Why do you ask?"

"I can't really say. Just curiosity."

The sergeant gave Sanford a doubtful look, and Sanford returned a hard and challenging stare.

"By all appearances, Sergeant, there's been an attempt to abduct my daughter. I think I'm allowed more than normal curiosity."

"Of course, sir. I understand, but I really don't see –"

"You don't see what, Sergeant? Was this man working alone? Is there someone else out there right now? Can I expect another attempt tomorrow? Next week? I haven't heard you ask whether I would like some kind of protective surveillance for my daughter. Or are you expecting me to do that myself?"

"I'm sorry sir. I didn't mean –"

"Yes Sergeant. I know exactly what you didn't mean. You didn't mean for me to find out anything substantive. You didn't mean to give me any impression that you were concerned about my daughter's welfare. Well, you can hide all you want behind the integrity of your investigation as a means of keeping me in the dark. Fine. I'll just be forced to take matters into my own hands."

"I have to warn you sir about interfering –"

"No Sergeant. It's me who's warning you."

Giving Nokes no chance to reply, Sanford turned and left the detachment.

Sanford returned to Joe's place and spent fifteen minutes fussing Reggie, the hero of the hour. Reggie barked and growled in delight, and was more than pleased to receive a reward, a large helping of his favourite kibble.

It took longer than Sanford expected, but eventually his cellphone rang.

"Sanford".

"Oh, hello Mr. Sanford. This is Inspector Halloran in Stanley Falls. Would it be convenient for me to come and see you now?"

"Yes, that would be convenient. I'm at Joe Stanton's place. Do you know where that is?"

"Yes sir. I'll be there in five minutes."

And indeed, it was less than five minutes later when an unmarked, dark blue car pulled into Joe's drive. Sanford was there to meet the car – a senior policewoman at the wheel, the window wound down, and Sanford standing too close for the door to open. He stood there for about twenty seconds, in the position of dominance familiar to all police, long enough for the message of his serious annoyance to get through.

"Come around the back, Inspector", Sanford said pleasantly once the officer managed to climb out of her car. "We can sit outside and talk."

Halloran didn't make the mistake of trying to engage in small talk as they walked the short distance to Joe's large picnic table, which shared a concrete slab with several cushioned lounging chairs. Sanford took a seat at the table, and waved Halloran to sit opposite him.

Sanford judged that Inspector Halloran was in her early fifties. She was tallish, had a wiry build, fine features, pale blue eyes, and time had applied artistic brushings of grey to the ends of the short curls peeking from beneath her cap. She projected an air of confidence and competence.

"I want to apologize for Sergeant Nokes. That's certainly not the way I expect my officers to behave when something like what you've experienced has occurred."

Sanford nodded acknowledgement. "Is there anything you can tell me that would give me some assurance that my daughter is not in danger now?"

"Unfortunately, no, there isn't. At the moment, we know nothing about who hired the suspect, assuming he was working alone, or what exactly they had in mind. We don't know yet who the suspect is, but based on his reported behaviour it certainly looks as though he's not a novice. So, he almost certainly has form and once we find out who he is we should be able to get much more information from Metro Police and the OPP central office. That might help us figure out just what's going on here. In the meantime, can I ask whether there is anywhere away from Stanley Falls where your daughter could stay for a few days?"

"No. There are her grandparents, but they're old and infirm and suffering their own loss at the moment. If this charlie was able to find us here, then someone else could certainly find her there. I'm really interested in what suggestions you might have."

"I understand what you're saying, sir. Unfortunately, there's a limited amount we can do. We can have a conspicuous patrol pass by your house every hour, but that's about the extent of it. We just don't have the personnel for more hands-on protection."

Sanford fixed an unblinking gaze on Halloran for several seconds, his face set grimly. "If I have to take measures myself, I will do so. I hope you understand that."

"Yes, sir. I understand fully. I would ask, though, what you might consider as measures."

"Well, for example, if I have to hire my own protective detail, I will do that. And I want to make it clear that I will do whatever is needed to protect my family."

"Fully understood sir. I would do the same. I do feel that I need to caution you about excessive –"

"Please Inspector! Neither of us is an idiot! Of course, I don't wish to kill or injure anyone! But neither will I tolerate the threat of that happening to me or to Julia! It seems pretty clear to me that whoever is behind this is playing a serious game. So I'm certainly not going to stand by meekly if it looks like something irreversible might be about to happen."

"I fully understand your concern and your position, Mr. Sanford. I want to be sure that you understand mine."

"Yes, I think we understand each other, Inspector."

Halloran then moved the conversation off onto more general, and safer, topics. They talked for about twenty minutes, then Halloran made to rise, passing Sanford her card, and offering her hand.

When she had left, Sanford pondered the discussion, then returned to Anne's place. He wanted to spend more time with her, make sure she was all right after the trauma of the near abduction, and be there when Julia awoke from her nap. The remainder of the evening passed quickly.

# Twenty-two

Although Sanford was unsettled, he spent much of the next day thinking and planning. Aware now that threats to his daughter of physical violence and kidnapping were shown to be all too real, he pondered anxiously what to do. Working on the Alberta oil rigs, he had encountered assholes, head cases, guys whose primary source of pleasure was sadism and dominance, and he learned that sometimes the only way to be sure that they kept their distance, and that he kept himself out of their crosshairs, was to find an appropriate occasion to beat the shit out of them. Being large and strong, as he was, he could do this, but violence alone simply did not suffice, since it is a last resort, even among testosterone-charged assholes. He found that he had to learn the physical and psychological lingo of street encounters. There were rituals – routines – that engaged just the right amount and kinds of de-escalation, resistance, threat, belligerence, at just the right time for a given situation and avoided the unnecessary aggro that could follow from under- or over-reaction. He learned them all, and played the game such that the roustabout assholes generally left him alone.

It was possible for him to behave that way then, because he had only himself to look out for, and he had discovered that he could handle himself well. The presence of Julia swept all those old blunt rules aside, and placed him in new territory, where he didn't know the rules, assuming there were any, and where the stakes were much higher. Although vague, the threat he faced on behalf of them both was real, and he needed urgently to find a way of cutting through, seeing beyond, that vagueness.

Anne and Julia had been engaged in another project since just after breakfast, leaving Sanford to take stock. By mid-afternoon, Sanford continued in the fraught musings raised by the events of the previous day, and he had the feeling that he was making little or no progress. When his cellphone vibrated, he reached for it eagerly, welcoming this diversion and potential relief. It was Conway.

"Hello Mr. Conway."

"Mr. Sanford. I'm in Stanley Falls. We need to talk. Can you give me directions to your place please?"

Rather than air his surprise and ask questions that Conway probably would brush aside anyhow, Sanford just gave him directions to Joe's place.

"I'll see you shortly then, Mr. Sanford", and the connection was gone.

Conway arrived in less than five minutes. Before Conway could get into the story on why he was in Stanley Falls, Sanford briefed him on what had happened. Conway listened intently. Sanford explained that he had to go across the road pretty much right away to arrange details of the evening meal with Anne. He asked Conway where he was staying, and found out that Conway had booked himself into a motel on the edge of town.

"If it's not too late to do so, you can ask the motel to cancel the booking and then you can move in here. We have three spare bedrooms. I assume you'll only be passing on the motel costs to me anyhow, and if you were here that would give us all the time to talk that we would need, without anyone wondering about the guy checked into the motel."

Conway agreed right away, which surprised Sanford somewhat, since he expected more coaxing to be needed. Conway pulled out a card and his cellphone, called the motel, did some grovelling and apologizing, and managed to have his reservation cancelled, promising to come and collect all his things immediately.

"Let me show you where you'll sleep. When you return you can settle in right away. I might not be here when you get back, but I'll be away only a few minutes."

Conway nodded agreement, Sanford indicated that the door would be unlocked, and they both left.

When Sanford got to Anne's place, he found that Julia and Anne had undertaken a cookie-baking marathon, and Anne was covering the home stretch on her own. She was piling cookies onto wire racks to cool, and related to Sanford, through an indulgent smile, that the last few days' excitement, the heat in the kitchen, and the sugar hit from a few trial cookies had pushed Julia over the edge, and that she was napping.

Even as Anne spoke, Sanford noticed that the events of the past two days, good and bad, had borne down on her, and that she looked tired. Sanford observed her closely, but unobtrusively. Apart from appearing tired, she seemed to be back to her old self, and when he asked her if she wanted company, she said no, that things were fine, and gave a deprecating laugh. Sanford checked with her about dinner, which he had already insisted they would have at his place, and it was clear that she was relieved all over again at not having to worry about a meal. He told her that it would be informal, that she should just come over whenever Julia was awake, and he said that there would be someone else at dinner – a colleague from Toronto he had invited to the country for a few days' rest.

Sanford then went back to Joe's place to await Conway's return.

Ten minutes later, Conway knocked politely then immediately entered carrying a small suitcase, and a black bag that evidently held a computer and probably an assortment of notebooks. He and Sanford nodded wordlessly to each other, indicating Conway's intent, and Sanford's acknowledgement, that Conway would stow his suitcase and be right back.

When Conway returned to the kitchen, he was dressed in jeans and a short-sleeved shirt. Sanford pre-empted any business discussions by stating that according to his best guess they would be eating dinner in about forty-five minutes, they being him and Conway, Sanford's daughter Julia, and the woman across the road, Anne Ferguson, who had been looking after Julia. Sanford said that they knew Conway would join them for dinner, but all they knew about him was that he was one of Sanford's colleagues. Conway nodded.

"Anything I can do to help with dinner?" Conway asked.

"No, I don't think so, but help yourself to some wine."

Sanford made the initial preparations, and Julia and Anne arrived a few minutes later. Introductions were made, soft drinks and wine were opened, and the initial probing questions drifted into a comfortable conversation. Sanford then got the cooking itself started.

At Sanford's suggestion, they ate outside, since it had been another fine day, and was now a warm afternoon sliding into what promised to be a long and placid evening. Anne asked Conway what he did, and he answered in a way that gave enough specifics to appear responsive but without really saying anything. The discussion over dinner indicated that Conway was a true artist when it came to posing interesting questions that elicited interesting information. They sat around for a while after finishing, their postures and faces mirroring the satiated languor of the evening, and engaging in desultory conversation. When Sanford rose to collect the plates and carry them into the kitchen, Conway was right on his heels, something that evidently impressed Anne, who was able to sit quietly while someone else did the after-dinner work that she was so accustomed to having to do. When that was done, Sanford fed Reggie, who had been waiting quietly next to his friend Julia, and they all watched the dog enjoy his meal as much as they had enjoyed theirs.

"Daniel and I have a few things to discuss", Sanford said at length. "I hope you don't mind."

"No, not at all", Anne protested. Julia suggested that she and Anne do some weeding in Joe's garden, and they set off to do that. Sanford and Conway went back inside, quickly washed up the dishes, then moved to Joe's den where they could push the door to, without fully closing it, indicating politely that they wanted privacy.

Conway's first few statements surprised Sanford.

"I've had a look into these two guys, Harold Sanford and Charles Jeffers. I'll use Harold's first name to avoid any confusion between you and him. Harold is, or was, both crafty and devious. There seems to be nothing in his life that one could call clear or straightforward. Apart from a very brief period as a salesman for Procter & Gamble, I can't find any indication of who else he worked for. If, indeed, he ever worked for anyone else. My suspicion is that he was always a lone wolf, and he must have been a very subtle one, because he left hardly any prints behind him."

"But there were payments from him to his wife, Aileen."

"I have to accept your statement on that Mr. Sanford. But I can't find any record of money moving through any arrangement that had the name Harold Sanford associated with it."

Sanford shook his head in disbelief. "Not that long ago, just a couple of weeks, there was a sum of money transferred to me on Aileen's death, and the lawyer's letter indicated that this was being done on instructions from Harold Sanford." As he was speaking, Sanford fished out Harold's letter and the lawyer's letter and passed them on to Conway. Conway looked at them briefly.

"And how, precisely, did the money come to you?" he asked.

"It was via a banker's draft."

"And did that come to you through the mail, through a bank?"

"No. It came as part of the content of a safe deposit box." Even as he said this, Sanford recognized how odd that method of transfer was.

"None of this surprises me", Conway said. "Somebody, and we have no idea who, put a banker's draft into a safe deposit box that was then delivered to you on instructions from someone who could have been that same person, or somebody else. And the draft would have shown your name, the name 'Harold Sanford' typed out, and most likely an illegible signature. I doubt that it was drawn on any account. Probably it was just purchased in cash, transferred to the bank from somewhere. All of this might well have been done by Harold Sanford, but equally it could have been anybody."

"But, he would need identification in order for the bank to complete a transaction like that."

"Yes, he would, which is why I think it might well have been Harold Sanford. But, one needs to bear in mind that there are some excellent forgers out there."

"But why would anybody go to all that trouble?"

Conway looked directly at Sanford. "I think that's just the kind of person Harold is, or was."

"Hang on!" Sanford interjected. "Do you think he's dead or not?"

"I really don't know."

"Do you think that's what Harold wants people to think, that he wants everybody to be in doubt? Because he always wanted to be in a position where nobody ever knew what he was up to?"

"That's exactly what I think, and why I think it."

"Is there any evidence he was actually doing that?" Sanford asked, then realized it was a silly question, answering himself before Conway could, by saying "Of course there's no evidence because he wanted there never to be any."

They both nodded, having reached a common plateau of understanding.

"If he is dead, surely there will be records of his death", Sanford observed, as though toying with a loose end, and then they both said in unison "but there are some excellent forgers out there".

"So we've hit a dead end", Sanford said flatly.

"Yes. We've hit a dead end. On the basis of evidence. But on the basis of rumour there's a lot of information one can tap into."

"Rumour?" Sanford asked in some surprise.

"This business is a shadow business", Conway began. "Usually, the only records left behind about these people and their dealings are those produced by the police. Where the police reach dead ends, or in the cases where the police never become involved, there are no records. But the shadow world is well-populated, and those people notice things. That's information of a sort, and there's a market for it. Knowing who's doing what is sometimes a clue as to why they're doing it, or the starting point for deducing why they're doing it. People in the shadow world do things for reasons that generally involve money directly, or the means to acquire money, and that's the basis for the rumour information market. If I'm a shady character doing something on the quiet, and some other shady character learns this, he'll want to know what I'm doing and why. Maybe that somebody else has missed a trick, or maybe he can whisk something valuable out from under my nose, or maybe he can prevent something being whisked out from under his own nose. Harold is known out there as a very smooth operator, and because those rumours exist and persist, I'm inclined to believe that he's been flying successfully under the legal radar for many years."

"So he hasn't been a salesman all these years?"

"Oh, he probably has done all the things that salesmen do. He probably has made sales, and has had products or goods delivered. But that's not how he's been making most of his money, and it seems that he really has made, or come into, a great deal of money over the years."

Sanford made a gesture of incomprehension, indicating that Conway should elaborate.

"Well, I would say that Harold has probably combined, very artfully and very successfully, the roles of swindler, embezzler, and blackmailer, and has used techniques that many business people would recognize."

Sanford pondered all this for a good three or four minutes.

"Are you saying that he might in fact be dead, or are you saying that he might not be dead?"

"I'm saying that he might be either. If he really is dead, then the records of his death might be telling the truth. But if he is really just 'dead' on paper, then he has chosen to be 'dead' for some very good reason."

"What kind of reason?"

"Well", Conway continued, "he might have got himself into a difficult corner, and the easiest way out was to 'die'. Or he might have started afresh as a different person. Or he might just have left the game completely and started a new life somewhere."

"Which do you think it is?"

"I'm inclined to believe", Conway said slowly, "that it's some combination".

"What leads you to that conclusion?" Sanford asked.

"Ah! This brings us to Charles Jeffers."

"Charles Jeffers?" Sanford said in surprise.

"You did ask me to dig into Charles Jeffers, find out whatever I could. I have to say that it surprised me too when what I dug up gradually led me to the view that there is, or was, some kind of link between Harold and Jeffers."

"What kind of link?"

"An agreement between thieves, it would seem. Among whom, as we know, there is no honour."

"So, you think there might have been some kind of business link between them?" Sanford asked.

"Yes, but let me sketch what I've found out about Jeffers. He seems to be a con man and blackmailer. He wasn't ever into the really big time, apparently, although there were three occasions when a fairly big prize was involved, the police had a good deal of evidence, but Jeffers came up with an alibi in each case that was unbreakable and completely believable. So he got off, in all three of those cases. I know nothing about just what Harold and Jeffers might have got up to together, but apparently there was something, if one can believe the rumours. It looks as though it was an arrangement for something more than a one-time job, that they worked together for months, or maybe a couple of years. But then something happened. Suddenly they weren't an item any longer."

"When do you think this breakup happened?"

Conway tapped his pen on the desk, pensively, Sanford thought, and was surprised at his own frivolous wordplay. "It seems to have happened just about the time you received this", and Conway waved the lawyer's letter Sanford had handed him a few minutes earlier.

"What sort of something?" Sanford asked.

"Not sure. Something very significant, for both Harold and Jeffers, but it was significant for each of them for different reasons."

Sanford waited.

"This is really in the realm of supposition now", Conway began in caveat fashion. "Harold and Jeffers likely planned a big job together. They likely carried it off successfully. But then something went sour, and it looks as though Jeffers was cut out of his share. Beyond that there might be more. I can't tell. Then Harold 'died' or disappeared. From that time on, the rumour mill has gone completely quiet on Harold. Jeffers was still out there screaming blue murder to whoever in the shadow world would listen, but then he too went quiet a few weeks ago."

"Why would someone like Harold just give away a large lump sum to me, when he had no need to do that? It seems completely out of character, not credible at all."

"No? Look at his letter. It's a masterpiece. A remorseful man's attempt to make amends for how he had wronged a woman. It reads like the account of a confused, humble, and contrite soul who has scraped together a lifetime bounty that he should have made available to his good woman over the years. I can't think of a better way to generate fog, create an image out there in the shadow world of an ordinary chap struggling to do the right thing."

"If he's viewed as such a slippery character, who would believe this?"

"Some people would", replied Conway, "but anyway it's grist for the rumour mill – it adds uncertainty, doubt, distortion."

"But a quarter million dollars –" Sanford began.

"Means nothing to Harold", Conway interrupted, completing the sentence.

Sanford considered all this for a moment. "Okay", he said. "This is a great deal of background. It's also information that demolishes the last of any preconceptions I had about Harold. What about the attempt to abduct Julia a few days ago?" Sanford walked through those events in a bit more detail for Conway.

Conway thought about it for a minute. "That one's not clear at all. Perhaps it's Jeffers trying to get some kind of reaction out of Harold. She's his granddaughter, after all."

"But you said Jeffers went quiet a few weeks ago", Sanford challenged. "In addition to that, Harold has never shown any interest in Julia whatsoever." Sanford expressed this with some venom, and he wondered whether Conway had missed the phrase in Harold's letter making it clear that Julia and Harold were completely unrelated. But Sanford just let it go, thinking that it might be best to leave the matter to one side for the time being.

Conway shrugged. "Thinking about it a little more", he began, "this attempted abduction job looks botched from several points of view. For an abductor to be foiled so completely like that indicates an almost total lack of planning and detailed information. Looks like the guy thought it would be a pushover, and that any hitches could be overcome by applying a little muscle." He paused here, obviously giving it more thought. "In fact, it looks odd. The guy the police have arrested seems a bit dim, and likely he'll start talking pretty soon. I would bet, however, that he has no idea who really is involved. If Jeffers is behind it, he's likely organized it through a middleman. But then again, if Jeffers is involved, I would have expected a slicker operation. In fact, I would have expected the abduction to be successful. So, maybe it's just a try-on by somebody, not Jeffers, who thought he could screw some cash out of you. It's strange, I have to admit."

Sanford was trying to work out a rationale in his head, based on Conway's speculations. He knew, or was pretty sure, that Jeffers was not involved, because he knew for a fact that Jeffers was dead long before the attempted abduction took place. But, he couldn't tell Conway that, nor could he tell anyone else, since it would lead inevitably to an investigation, all their lives being dragged publicly through the mud, and to what purpose? To deliver some semblance of process or justice, of closure, to Jeffers? Jeffers had been a complete prick for whom decay beneath a manure pile was already far too generous a fate. As he thought about it, Sanford began leaning more and more toward Conway's suggestion of just an opportunistic nab, that there was incompetence behind this opportunism, and that having failed so ridiculously, they wouldn't try again. In any case, Sanford intended to put in place visible and prominent barriers, their exact nature yet to be decided upon, to make it clear that anybody mounting a second attempt was likely to be hurt.

"What will you do now?" Sanford asked.

"I propose", Conway began, "with your agreement, to keep digging for dirt on Jeffers. If there's more information on a link between Harold and Jeffers, I want it. If digging around sends a message out into the shadow world that this search for information is serious, we might even see some nibbles that could lead to other hard information."

"I agree", Sanford said.

He knew that a search to detect involvement by Jeffers was pointless, but he felt that he had a part to play in this charade, to bring things to a conclusion, to wrap everything up. He had no doubt that there would be loose ends that could not be tied off, but what else was new in life?

# Twenty-three

Conway stayed two days in Stanley Falls, then he returned to Toronto. Sanford and Conway had two other heads-together sessions before Conway left, and Sanford decided he liked this somewhat odd investigator.

True to his word, Conway kept digging, and a stream of bits and pieces was directed Sanford's way. Nobody knew where Jeffers was, and speculation started surfacing that he had been eliminated. The would-be abductor also turned out sometimes to go by the name Damion Plumb, something that soon unleashed a small raft of stupid jokes about jam, toast, and whatnot. Conway soon found connections between Plumb/Wakelin and other small-time hoods, all of whom started looking like laughable walk-on characters in a comic story of cops and robbers. The *who* and *why* of the attempted abduction remained unclear, and Conway thought his initial speculation was looking more and more likely, although he kept digging. Three days after he had left Stanley Falls, Conway sent Sanford an email saying that he was halting his efforts to trace more details on Jeffers and on the details of Julia's attempted abduction. He was not coming up with anything new, he said, and he didn't expect to come up with anything new. Conway said he would keep an eye on things, meaning a few hours a week making the usual rounds of contacts, and that he would send his invoice soon.

Sanford's world relaxed somewhat, at least in regards to Julia's safety. His previous world, the world he had known for as far back as he could remember, lay in ruins. The people closest to him, and for whom he had the strongest feelings, were not what he had believed they were. He himself was adrift, and in terms of family identity, well, he simply didn't have one. But Sanford refused to let himself be dragged down by this.

He and Maxwell spoke regularly, Maxwell always telling him that his family had priority. The days went by quickly. Julia obviously enjoyed her time with her new friends, and was delighted when Sanford presented her with a new bicycle. It was blue and matched her shorts.

Four days before they were to leave for Italy, Sanford suddenly suggested that he and Julia head off to Toronto.

"I just realized that we need to buy you some luggage."

"I can use one of Mommy's suitcases."

"Absolutely not! A world traveller can't go around begging luggage from other people. Let's start off right. Besides, maybe we'll have time for a trip to the aquarium as well."

Judging from the gleeful hopping about, the chance of an aquarium visit clinched a trip to Toronto, and put the final kibosh on borrowed luggage. They had an early breakfast, jumped in Sanford's car, and drove off into the morning.

Julia was animated all the way to Toronto, partly because of a trip to the aquarium, partly because she suddenly realized that the luggage she was about to acquire would need to be shown to her new friends, probably also because of the dawning awareness that a big and exciting trip was about to happen, and possibly because of some faint, emerging primal urge to shop.

Picking luggage turned out to be an excruciating pleasure. Julia had no inkling that there were so many designs and colours of suitcases, and in three different shops, bags were dragged across the room to be placed next to other bags, a binary selection was made, then other candidates were dragged to sit next to one another. This went on for over an hour, while Sanford looked on indulgently, being in no particular rush. She finally chose a brilliant blue child's suitcase that had fifteen or twenty national flags printed onto it at different angles, like old-time luggage stickers. This treasure was deposited in the car, and they then headed off to the aquarium.

It was another world, and Julia pressed her face to the windows, behind which there was marine life of all sorts floating, hovering, darting, or drifting through the crystal-clear water.

At four o'clock they headed back toward Stanley Falls, even though that meant struggling through heavy traffic. Julia was fired up on nervous energy from the day's action, but Sanford knew that when they reached Joe's place there would barely be enough time for a light supper before one small bundle of exhaustion would need to be carried to her bed.

Sanford didn't notice, just after he had entered the expressway on his way to Toronto, the olive green Dodge Durango in the eastbound lanes travelling the opposite way, nor did he notice the same car travelling west at about six thirty when he was returning home. When they pulled into Joe's drive, Julia was already fading fast, and had the energy to drink only half a glass of milk before the lights went out.

During the past several weeks, Anne had discovered the novelty of email, and had practised quite a bit by sending messages to Sanford. She had sent another one during the day, noting that a car had driven slowly past Joe's place several times, and she passed on the plate number. But Sanford had to feed Reggie, being famished himself he had to make something to eat, and had still some planning to do for the trip to Italy, so he didn't catch up to Anne's email until the following morning.

# Twenty-four

When Sanford finally read Anne's email the next day, an alarm sounded in his head. He forwarded the car licence number to Conway, thought about the potential risk briefly, then shelved the matter. He had the euros he would need for the trip, their hotels were booked, Sanford had put himself through a crash course on tourist Italian, a new passport had arrived for him, one that included Julia, he had picked up two good tourist guides on northern Italy, and he had begun to lay out the things he would need to take. Once their plane left the ground, he felt that he could put local concerns behind him.

Sanford had been priming Julia on how to be a good traveller, and he had helped her choose the clothes she wanted to take. He was a bit taken aback at her initial resistance to this, and he thought he could read something surprising in her face, such as "A woman doesn't need help from a man in deciding what and how to pack". This was so much like Helen and it brought before him images of a past that was now far in the distance. Regardless of whether his impression was based on something real or imagined, he had to smile. In stark contrast to this was Julia's toiletry kit. He had bought her a small toiletry bag surreptitiously when they were in Toronto, and when he gave it to her and explained what it was for, she spent the best part of a day repeatedly packing her personal things in it and then unpacking them.

And then the big day arrived. Stephen Maxwell had offered to collect Julia and Sanford and deliver them to the airport, and the more Sanford attempted to decline the offer politely, the more insistent Maxwell became. He arrived about ten thirty, and they set off for Toronto just after eleven. By eleven thirty, Maxwell had become Uncle Stephen, much to his delight. Maxwell pulled into one of the nicer, smaller hotels in the airport strip at about one o'clock, and said they were going to have a light lunch, no arguments.

When they had finished a light but leisurely lunch, Maxwell drove the short distance to the terminal car park, helped Julia out of the car in a gallant flourish, and they headed off to the departure area. Their flight would leave at six o'clock so they were in good time, and Maxwell wished them *bon voyage* before starting back to his car. A last wave from far down the cavernous building, and then he was gone.

Julia had talked all the way from Stanley Falls, having more than a little encouragement from Uncle Stephen, and the palaver of checking their bags and making it through security and into the waiting area near the gate did nothing to dampen her loquacity.

"Are we sitting together, Daddy?"

"How long will it take us to get there, Daddy?"

"Won't it be the middle of the night when we get there, and what will we do then?"

"Will we be able to go shopping right away?"

"Do they have ice cream in Italy?"

"Who is Maria, Daddy?"

"Will I like Maria?"

"Did I pack my blue shorts, Daddy? I can't remember."

Sanford diverted the conversation away from a stream-of-consciousness question-and-answer approach, by beginning a narrative on where they were going, what they would see, what they could do, and what would be different. The business of boarding the plane, watching all the fuss and bother of people trying to get settled in the right seats, provided Sanford the usual entertainment, and judging from her suppressed giggling this had brushed off onto Julia. But anticipation grew as the preparations for takeoff were completed, and then the great roar of the engines and being thrust back into her seat fanned Julia's excitement, and the exhilaration as the huge bird finally took to the air left her in open-mouthed wonder. Sanford had arranged for them to have window and middle seats in a bulkhead row, he had Julia take the window seat, and she was clearly enthralled at the bumpy climb, the plane banking to take up the long easterly run, but especially at seeing clouds up close for the first time, watching them race past, over, and around the wing. She gripped Sanford's hand in that delicious, slightly fearful exhilaration of something entirely new, something having the power, both physical and metaphorical, to transport one suddenly into a different world.

She smiled broadly at Sanford.

"Oh Daddy! I think I'm really going to like this!"

For almost half an hour she was glued to the window, watching the first layer of fluffy clouds fall beneath her and begin looking like a peculiar albino landscape far below, then passing through the next layer of clouds, and eventually looking up to find that the sky above was no longer bright blue but a very dark blue, almost black. The drinks service began, Sanford ordered two white wines and an apple juice, poured a small amount of white wine for Julia and shushed her conspiratorially. They clinked plastic glasses and toasted "To Italy!" The meals were delivered, Julia ate most of hers, but then within about ten minutes she fell into that fathomless sleep of emotionally exhausted happy children, who are sometimes known as "tired little teddy bears".

Sanford leaned back in his seat. He had something to read, and he also had some pondering to do. But his mind kept roving, uncomfortably, obsessively, over the past weeks and months. His life had been overturned, his past had become unknown, wreathed in heavy cloud, and lurking behind it all was the black reality he had uncovered at Joe's farm.

Realistically, he expected none of this to be resolved during the present trip. He would make the acquaintance of someone from Joe's past, Maria. Where any of this might lead, if indeed it could lead anywhere, Sanford had no idea.

From Sanford's review of Joe's personal notes, Joe had met Maria during a trip to Italy in his youth. She had obviously meant something to Joe, if only as a summer fling. He had been a young man, transferring himself willingly from his element and into a new culture. Knowing Joe, he would have grabbed this tree in both hands and shaken hard to see what fell out. The sharp tang of new surroundings, the feast of new settings, both urban and rural, that were steeped in history, the intellectual shiver of a new language refracting and stretching his mind, these were things Joe would have taken the time to explore. Turning these thoughts over in his mind, Sanford had experienced a small pang of expectancy. This was the special kind of time that had never been available to Sanford during any of his previous business trip forays into Italy, where the use of pretty much every second had been dictated by commercial exigency. He was determined to use the present trip to close that gap. And if there was anything more he could learn about Joe's past, he would do that as well. But Joe's trip there had been a long time ago, and Sanford had quite low expectations of learning anything new about his friend.

Looking around the now-darkened plane, Sanford asked himself what he really expected to get from this trip. He had thought about that often and long enough, and felt certain that he wanted the trip to be, would make it be, a pivot point for Julia and for him, a point where they left the past behind and moved into their future. The impressions of Italy that he carried back from previous trips, a place of sunshine, animation, and zest for life, would be, he hoped, something they could take their time exploring in some depth, giving them a benchmark, a reference point, a turning point, for both their lives.

Simple ideas, dressed in elaborate costume. Put more bluntly, he needed to find any clues that would help fill in the gaps in his own past, gaps that he didn't know existed until a few weeks ago. He needed to get Julia and himself out of the rubble of the recent past and onto a new track to the future.

From this musing about the immediate future, Sanford had fallen into a light doze, and when he awoke a pale purple stripe defined the horizon through the window. They were about two hours out of Milan. Sanford switched on his reading light, opened the book he had brought, and promptly dozed off again.

They passed through an area of turbulence, and it jostled him in continuous and irritating regularity.

# Twenty-five

A week before the flight, Sanford had sent Maria a note, necessarily in English, using the address he had found in Joe's little address book, which Sanford had found at the back of a drawer in Joe's bedside table. There had been no time for a reply to reach him, he knew this when he sent the letter, but better some warning than none at all. He had told Maria the name of the hotel in Genoa where he would be staying and the day he would be arriving, and said that he would attempt to contact her once he was in the hotel. He was prepared for disappointment, since there was no guarantee that Maria was at the same address, even in the same city, or that if she was she would be interested in seeing Sanford. But he was convinced that he had to try, that this might be the only place remaining where he could learn more about Joe. Sanford had decided that on their return to Toronto he would ask Conway to have one more go at unravelling Sanford's past, and that he would then close the book on the whole matter, regardless of how little they might find.

They made the tight connection at Milan for the flight to Genoa, and Sanford was now watching his daughter closely as the plane from

Milan banked over the Ligurian Sea, aiming at Genoa's airport lying on the waterfront to the west of the city. Above, the sky boasted its early morning cloudlessness. Below, the sea radiated a silent, irresistible aquamarine. The city revealed itself as being almost cephalopod, flowing into deep ravines and gullies, and, wherever it could do so, sliding upward over the steep hills that rose from the sea. The whole panorama and what it presented – the colours, the delightful jumble of buildings, the exotic-looking trees and shrubs that barely managed to cover the rocky hills – this was all new to Julia, and she was clearly trying to take in every detail.

In contrast to this quiet contemplation of his own daughter, Sanford revisited, briefly, the thoughts and unanswered questions that had kept resurfacing in his mind overnight. Why had he been blindsided by the two people closest to him on who he really was and on his background? When should he explain these things to Julia, something that surely he must do? There was no doubt in his mind that he had received a very caring upbringing, one that was filled by more love and guidance than those of many of the young people he had known. And yet, the way he viewed Aileen and Joe had now been cast into deep shade. How would this resolve itself over the coming months? How would his view of Aileen and Joe change? Both of them must have known what the withholding of that information would mean for him. Were they hoping that, somehow, he never would find out? Did they have a plan for explaining it all to him eventually? Was there something in the past they were trying to protect him from? Was there something that prevented them from explaining his past to him? If so, what could that possibly have been?

The plane bumped a little on the morning thermals, and the pilot turned on to the approach for landing. As they lost altitude, the sea below gradually was transformed from a deep, flat, mysterious, and psychologically soothing blue, to a two-dimensional surface hinting at features, and then to water, and waves, and small boats. Features on the land side rushed past at increasing speed, and then the tires thumped and squeaked against *terra firma*, and soon they were stopped at the gate. Unloading from the smallish regional plane began almost immediately, and before they knew it Sanford and Julia were walking down the stairway in bright, humid morning air. Claiming their luggage took barely ten minutes. They were soon in a taxi, heading east along the coast, since Sanford had asked the driver to follow a route from which they could see as much of the city as possible, even if it meant that the trip took a bit longer. The back windows of the cab were down a little. The light, the sounds, occasionally the smells, and above all the history that seeped from every pore of the city wafted into the car and over them. Despite being tired and in a state of some circadian confusion, Julia was transfixed by all that was new, that had to be absorbed and understood.

Sanford had chosen a good small hotel off *Via Cairoli*, and had opted for a large suite, casting financial caution to the winds. They soon pulled up outside the hotel, the taxi driver's Mediterranean energy being infectious as he unloaded the luggage, flashed them a big smile, and wished them a pleasant stay in Genova.

"Well, here we are, young lady", Sanford said past a big smile.

"Oh Daddy! It's really not like home at all!"

"No, that's why we came here. Let's get ourselves checked in, have a quick shower, change, and then go out and look around."

Half an hour later, they were back on the street, each wearing a new pair of blue shorts. Julia's grin reached both ears.

"What should we do first, Daddy", the "first" apparently indicating one item in what Julia evidently hoped would be a long list.

"I think we should go say hello to Giuseppe first, make our way down to the harbour, look at the galleon, take a bus tour, and then see about some lunch."

"Who's Giuseppe?"

"That's Giuseppe Garibaldi. I'll tell you about him."

And they set off along *Via Cairoli*, heading for the statue of Garibaldi in *Piazza de Ferrari*. All the way, Sanford explained what he knew about Italian history, and he was surprised at how much came back to him. Ever since he had read, years ago, a couple of books by Denis Mack Smith, he had been hooked, well and truly, on the details of nineteenth century Italian history. Sanford's enthusiasm was evidently finding a more-than-willing ear in Julia, as he related swashbuckling tales of Garibaldi in South America, sailing to the Orient, and the whole astonishing story of his "Thousand" in Sicily.

They walked around the statue of Garibaldi mounted on his horse. The large fountain hissed and spattered in the piazza, and Julia rattled off to Sanford a whole raft of questions about Garibaldi.

"What was he like?"

"Where did he live?"

"Was he ever in Toronto?"

"Will I be able to learn about him when I go to school?"

"Did he like blue shorts?"

Sanford's head snapped quickly around to Julia when he heard the last question, and he realized that he had been had by a five-year-old.

"You little scamp!" he exclaimed ruffling her hair, and they both broke into giggles. Sanford spent some time pointing out the buildings that surrounded them, focusing on their visual appeal rather than more local history baggage. They passed along *Via XXV Aprile*, walked up part of the hugely appealing slope of *Via Roma*, then cut through smaller streets circling back to *Via Garibaldi*. The morning sunlight flooded through the street toward them.

"Let's go to the harbour", Sanford suggested. They navigated more small streets, descending some fairly steep slopes, until suddenly they broke from deep shade into *Piazza Caricamento* and were struck by the smell of the sea. Their gaze was drawn naturally along the broad sweeping arc of the harbour that extended to their right.

*Neptune*, the Spanish galleon facsimile, drew an immediate squeal of delight, as it unveiled one vision of the seventeenth century before their eyes. It was an instant hit. They clambered over the ship, up and down stairs, and leaned over trying to see Neptune himself as the figurehead. They spent about an hour in the aquarium, but Sanford cut it short, promising they would return at least once. Outside, the little mock train offering a one-hour tour wouldn't leave for another half-hour, and Sanford convinced a slightly crestfallen Julia to settle for, instead, one of the large buses that would leave in ten minutes, knowing from past experience that the little trains were rough and noisy, and the commentary could be hard to hear. While the large bus could not cut through narrow passageways, areas that Sanford felt should be done on foot in any case, the tall windows and raised position in the seats gave them clear views of everything.

By this time, Julia was pretty clearly beginning to suffer from overload, so Sanford directed their steps back to a restaurant located in a small courtyard not far from their hotel. The quiet was relative, since the sounds of engaged Italian lives being lived spilled down onto them from the buildings all around.

Julia looked briefly at the menu, which meant nothing to her.

"Can we have spaghetti and meatballs?"

"No, not here. We'll have that somewhere else. Here we need to have pasta and seafood."

Sanford worked through the menu quickly. Julia had trouble deciding, but then agreed when Sanford suggested two plates of one of his favourites. Their food arrived, they tucked in, and Julia chattered away happily, oblivious to the red and pink stains that began appearing almost immediately on her white top. *What the hell,* Sanford said to himself, *we're on holiday.* In Julia's exuberance he recognized the signs of a hyper-charged youngster who was soon going to collapse. Just to be sure, he suggested a nice generous chunk of Genoese sponge cake for dessert. Even before they had finished their bottles of water, Julia was showing signs of fading.

After Sanford paid, he said "I think we'll go back to the hotel now and have a nice long nap." A quiet nod was her reply.

The hotel was a short distance away, but even so by the time they reached it Julia was beginning to pull heavily on Sanford's hand.

As they entered their suite, Sanford said "I have to go out for a short while, Julia, but I'll make sure the door is locked. Okay?"

Julia nodded tiredly, washed her face and hands distractedly, changed into pyjamas, and was asleep under just a sheet in less than fifteen seconds.

Sanford closed the bedroom door, pulled out his cellphone, moved to the far end of the suite, and retrieved the stored number he had entered into the phone from Joe's address book, hoping that it was still correct.

"Pronto."

"Hello Maria? This is Jim Sanford."

There was a long silence, and for a moment Sanford thought that maybe he had misjudged the thing entirely, that this woman, if she was Maria, had no idea who someone called Sanford was, that he would have to apologize for disturbing her and hang up, or that perhaps she had already disconnected.

"Hallo Gianni", she said in a quavery voice, and then burst into tears.

# Twenty-six

Sanford was taken aback. He didn't know quite what to say, neither to the crying woman, nor to the name Gianni, which seemed to be directed at him. Had he got the wrong person entirely? Had he got his wires dreadfully crossed and she thought he was somebody else? Was she just confused? Sanford began to doubt the entire project, but decided to forge ahead.

"I had hoped that we could meet, Maria", he ventured. "There are things we probably should talk about."

She didn't hang up. She didn't demand to know who was calling her. She was evidently bringing herself under control, and said, in English that was surprisingly free of accent, and through some suppressed sniffling "Yes." More sniffling. "When?"

"Right now is fine for me, Maria, if it's okay for you. Can I come and collect you in a taxi?" Although they had got this far, Sanford still had misgivings. It isn't every day that one is called by a stranger who hails from a distant city and says "We must meet". It still would not surprise him if she refused.

"A taxi? Oh. Yes", and she gave him her address. "I wait for you next to Ristorante Vittorio al Mare. I am wearing a green and white dress."

This sounded more promising. Sanford quickly consulted his large city map. "Good. I'll be there in about twenty minutes, Maria."

The taxi ride was a kaleidoscope of Genoese city scenes, each of which flitted past before Sanford had a chance to form anything other than a retinal impression of it, and soon they were on the *Corso Italia*. The taxi driver began rattling away in too rapid Italian for Sanford, once he learned that Sanford was from Toronto. The cabbie explained, Sanford was fairly sure, that he – the taxi driver – was originally from Calabria, and that he had two cousins in Toronto.

"Molto ricchi! Molto freddo!"

The only answer Sanford could come up with was "*Non oggi*".

The driver seemed suddenly alarmed. "*Cosa*?"

Sanford realized that he might have implied that financial disaster had just struck Toronto and that the cabbie's cousins were rich no longer.

"*Oggi non fa freddo a Toronto. Oggi fa caldo. Trenta gradi.*" But Sanford was by no means sure that he had said what he meant to, or even that what he had said made any sense at all.

The driver smiled in his mirror and waved a hand through the air in what was probably only one of a thousand possible hand signals. He continued to rattle on, as though he and this Torontonian had bonded for life.

They flew along the coast, and just when Sanford began to have doubts about where he was being driven, the driver wheeled off the *Corso*, and within a few seconds stopped next to an elegant-looking restaurant. A fairly tall, stylish, dark-haired woman, wearing a green and white dress, and carrying a tastefully matched handbag, stood waiting. She was trim, appeared to be about sixty, give or take, and her face bore a set of mature and rather attractive lines, reflecting what had probably been a reasonably happy life, rather than one battered by misfortune. Her dark eyes, pleasant mouth, good facial bone structure, Mediterranean colouring, and a smile that surfaced readily made her look very *simpatica*. She seemed vaguely familiar, but Sanford realized this had to be a "type" look since he knew nothing about her, except that there was some connection to Joe, and he certainly had never met her before.

Sanford asked the taxi driver to wait just a minute, and climbed out of the car.

"Would you mind coming now to my hotel, Maria? There's someone I want you to meet."

She looked puzzled, but agreed readily enough.

The return trip was accompanied by a continuing narrative from the driver, and appearing to try to decipher this flow helped Sanford mask the slightly uncomfortable feeling he had during the trip. It was probably fair enough. This woman Maria was a stranger to him, a complete stranger, the only link being through Joe. But Sanford had no idea what all that meant to her now, whether this meeting would turn out to be just one of those uncomfortable once-off duty visits that everyone is always pleased to see over. He looked across surreptitiously at Maria. Up close, her face spoke of strength and intelligence, a face that at one time, now decades past, likely would have radiated youthful beauty.

They arrived at the hotel soon enough, Sanford paid the driver, and they stepped out of the taxi.

"Can I buy you a cup of coffee, Maria?"

She smiled and said yes, and they moved toward a small café a couple of doors from the hotel, where there were several small tables in the street.

When they were settled, Sanford fussed a bit, not really knowing where to begin.

"I'm sorry I had to inform you of Joe's death in such an abrupt and impersonal way. I'm afraid that my letter to you must have been a shock."

"Yes. It was, a bit." She fiddled with her paper napkin, and a silence that was long, but felt quite natural, slowly extended between them.

"Could you tell me something about you and Joe?" Even as Sanford finished this question, he realized that only the few sentences in his letter to Maria told her anything about himself. He decided to rectify that later, since she seemed to have little hesitation in answering his questions.

She smiled, nodded once, and began fishing for something in her handbag.

The story came out easily. She and Joe had met in Rome. He was as green as they come, but there was a mutual attraction right away. His uncomplicated good looks, his apparent ability to pick up Italian at a ferocious rate, and his sense of humour that refused to remain stuck behind a linguistic barrier, made her realize that she wanted to know more about him. She and Joe had talked, and the discussion had stretched into lunchtime. They ate at a small café. Lunch had ended up lasting almost three hours. Between Maria's little bit of English, and Joe's little bit of Italian, they had got to know something of each other. From his sense of considerable doubt not half an hour ago, Sanford was now amazed that she was forthcoming with so much candour.

Maria had been talking to the middle distance for almost twenty minutes. She stopped and looked for a long time into Sanford's face.

"By the end of that day, I knew I was in love."

Here was indeed a new connection to Joe. Amid all the confusion and hurt that had entered Sanford's relationship to Joe since Joe had died, here was something fresh and positive.

Among the questions Sanford had that were crowding to get out, only the trivial ones passed the post first.

"What was Joe doing here? Where did he live? Was he just passing through Rome?"

She said that Joe had described himself then as an "innocent abroad", but said that she didn't really know how to interpret that until much later. "He wasn't doing anything here. He was a visitor. He wanted to see ruins. He wanted to get to know Rome."

There was another pause here.

She had pulled a picture out of her handbag, and as she laid it on the table now, her face melted into one of the most heartfelt and tender smiles Sanford had ever seen, but a smile tinged by great longing.

It was a picture of Joe. And Sanford had seen a picture very similar to it, very recently.

"He was twenty-three", Maria was saying. "He was the kindest, most gentle, and most intelligent man I had ever met. Nothing like most of the Italian boys I knew, boys who didn't grew up." A different kind of smile swept across her face. "My English is not good now", she said.

"Not true", Sanford objected. "Your English is very good. Where did you learn it?"

"Joe taught me English. It was one of his many gifts to me. A great gift for my working life."

"And I guess you taught Joe Italian?"

She shook her head. "No. Joe learned Italian himself, very quickly. Joe soon was able to speak Italian, how you say, *correntemente*."

"Oh. Yes. Fluently", Sanford said as the meaning of the Italian word suddenly became evident to him.

"Where you learn Italian?"

Sanford laughed. "I can't speak Italian. I know only a few phrases."

"Maybe", she said. "But I think you know the meaning here", and she pressed the knuckles of her right hand to her chest.

Sanford looked down again at the picture of a very young Joe, and suddenly he made the connection.

"Joe had a picture just like this. It was of you, wasn't it?"

Maria's face lit up. "He kept it!"

After a short delay, she continued. "Joe had a cheap camera. We took pictures of each other. It was one day at the *Altare della Patria*." She hesitated at the expression of incomprehension on Sanford's face. "Oh! Yes. He called it something different."

A pause.

A name came to Sanford, without him really knowing how. "Was it The Victor Emmanuel Monument?"

"Yes! You must be in Rome before", she said.

"Twice. On business. Three days altogether."

The waiter stopped as he was passing the table and said something to Sanford, in rapid Italian that was incomprehensible to him. Maria responded immediately, the waiter nodded, looked briefly at Sanford, then moved off. A moment later, the bill was set in front of him.

Although Sanford paid right away, they continued to sit at the table for a few minutes. It was a slack time and nobody appeared to mind.

"Where are you going after Genoa?" she asked, in neutral curiosity.

"Well, we're going to a number of other places, but all in Italy."

"We? You travel with your wife?"

From her expression, which suddenly clouded, Sanford realized that his face must have just telegraphed to her something unpleasant. "No Maria. My ex-wife died three weeks ago."

A hand went involuntarily to her mouth. "Oh! I'm sorry."

Sanford nodded without saying anything and tried to clear the sombre expression from his face.

"No. I'm here with my daughter." Even as he said it, he could feel the smile forming on his lips, but his frisson of happiness was quickly replaced by a sense of concern.

Maria's eyes were suddenly full of tears. But, in contrast to what Sanford took initially to be signs of grief, her face was radiant. She reached across the small table, and gripped both Sanford's hands tightly in hers.

"Oh Gianni! I didn't know I was a grandmother!"

# Twenty-seven

Sanford would look back on that scene later as one of the defining moments of his life.

The tenuous moorings his existence had regained in the past few weeks were suddenly cut again, and once more, he was far from a familiar anchorage.

Although the unwelcome senses of confusion and disorientation had returned in force, behind this there was something else. Huge blocks of puzzle were falling into place, each coming to rest with a thud, and generating personal seismic shocks as they did so. But these were shocks that precede stability, as when a five-ton keystone is dropped into the slot intended for it, and it fits like a glove, locking the entire arch into place and signalling, by an authoritative tremor, that an event of finality has indeed occurred.

Aileen.

The woman who had raised him. The woman who had showered onto him every last ounce of her love. The woman who could have no children. The woman he had known as his mother. Sanford realized now the context within which she had devoted her life to his upbringing, his welfare, his path into the world.

Maria.

His mother. The woman who bore him but for some reason had to give him up, and then stand aside in silence. Why this was, he had no idea, but he was certain that within the next few hours it would become clear.

Joe.

The person who had been Sanford's best friend. And the man who had been, the strong awareness just dawning on Sanford, his father. The man who had to keep all this a secret. Heart-rending thoughts rose within Sanford. Oh, Joe! If only I had known! If only we could have spoken, even though it might have been late in the game! If only! But he recognized now what Joe had done for him, what Joe had sacrificed. Sanford could feel tears running down his cheeks, tears of unbearable sadness, but also of unutterable joy.

"Maria", Sanford said in an unsteady voice. He looked at her kindly face through new eyes, they both rose from their chairs, he walked over to her, and enfolded her in a tight embrace.

Maria broke away first. "I have someone to meet", she said with determination. They both wiped their eyes, uttered pressure-relieving laughter, and turned toward the hotel.

They decided not to let Julia in on the entire story just yet, in fact they weren't going to let her in on any of it right away. Sanford would tell Julia that Maria was a good friend of Joe's and wanted to spend some time with Sanford and Julia, and talk a bit about Joe. She also would take them by the hand and lead them through the streets of Genoa, words that would acquire a new and much more personal meaning for Sanford.

When they entered Sanford's hotel suite, they found that Julia was still dead to the world. To Sanford, she looked angelic, as always. Her face was relaxed sweetly in sleep, the slight smudges beneath her eyes betraying the excitement of the morning and a night of inadequate rest on the plane. Her blond hair was splashed artistically across the plain cream pillows. Maria evidently had the same feelings, and the sight of Julia caused her immediately to begin dabbing at her eyes.

There was a small alcove off the main room of the hotel suite, and Sanford gestured that they might sit there. Seated in the sun, a warm breeze reaching in through the open window and plucking at their hair, they spent almost two hours in discussion that, to both of them, was unique and overwhelming.

During those two hours, the remaining missing elements of Sanford's life fell into place. Maria spoke of her first encounter with Joe in terms of a *colpo di fulmine*, and she said that looking back she was certain that they were both deeply in love within hours of their first meeting. They spent days and weeks together, visiting all the spots in Rome Joe wanted to see, and some he didn't know about. They spent days walking in the countryside outside Rome. It was all a haze, a connection between two people that was beyond the experience of either of them. They took day trips to the coast, trips inland to as far as Orvieto and Assisi.

In due course, Maria had become pregnant with Sanford, and as soon as she knew she was carrying a boy, she secretly always referred to him as Gianni, her little Gianni.

The dark clouds of trouble began gathering almost immediately. Maria knew that her family would explode if they found out. She would be sent away for the duration of the pregnancy. The baby, when he arrived, would be given up immediately for adoption. And that would be that.

Joe hatched all manner of schemes and floated them past Maria. She knew that none of them would work. She and Joe discussed the situation late into many nights. There was only one way forward that Maria could see – giving up the baby – and it was unpalatable to both of them. Marriage to Joe, a foreigner and not a Catholic, was a non-starter. Even to suggest it to her father would be little short of a declaration of war. The two of them were in anguish for what seemed an eternity.

Then Maria came up with an alternative. She would find "another job", somewhere out of Rome, *Torino* perhaps. She would move there and convince her family she was pursuing an employment opportunity too good to throw away. She would leave Rome, but the real reason would be to have the baby elsewhere, out of sight and out of harm's way. This plan, ostensibly looking to Maria's future as a graphic designer, certainly would cause frictions, of course. Her father would be against any plan that took her away from family, that left her susceptible to every cad who thought he might take a run at her. No. Maria's future was as the good wife to some worthy husband, someone her father could talk to, scrutinize, put through the wringer, before any decisions were made. But if the truth became known to the family, Maria felt certain that, after the fact, her mother would see the logic. Her mother, herself, had been caught in the "good wife" trap. They got along, even loved each other, her mother and father, but Maria's mother's life had been bereft of any future other than the family chores that had filled – overfilled – her time.

"What about the baby?" Joe had asked, unconvinced.

Through a flood of tears, Maria had said "You will have to raise him".

"Me? I'm not even a permanent resident in Italy."

"Not here", Maria had said, choking and sobbing. "In Canada."

Joe had lapsed into stunned silence.

Apparently they had argued things every which way, Joe trying to find the one path out of the labyrinth that they must have missed, that they surely had missed. But it always came back to just the two possibilities: adoption and loss of the baby for good, or Joe having custody.

"We did move away, but not to Torino. We moved to Moncalieri, near Torino. I have no relatives there, so it was a safe place. It wasn't easy. But we met nice people, kind people, and they helped us a lot. I had to deceive my parents, and that bothered me, but there was no other choice. You were born. Oh Gianni! You were such a beautiful baby! We registered the birth, got all the papers.

"And then the horrible day came. The day when you went to Canada with Joe. I thought I would never see you again, Gianni."

Sanford sat there, stunned, as a picture of what must have happened formed in his mind.

Suddenly, he knew.

He knew how this likely had all come about. The pieces all came together.

Joe had known Aileen from childhood and they had been neighbours for decades. They had become confidants, probably after Harold had abandoned Aileen. It was very likely that Aileen had confided in Joe about her barrenness on some dark occasion when she needed comfort. Then when Joe turned up with a baby, Aileen's instincts would have been given a powerful jolt. Sanford could imagine how it might have started off. Aileen offering to look after little Jim while Joe was off working long hours. Then a powerful bond slowly forming. Then Joe recognizing the drastic impact on Aileen that would result from any fundamental change in this arrangement. Joe simply let things ride, expecting that when the time was right all would be explained to Jim. Sanford had no proof that this was what had happened, but it fit, it felt completely right, and having this new view of the two most important people in his early life was something that took his breath away.

Sanford put his arm around Maria, around his mother's shoulders, and she wept silently.

"You probably wonder about the name Gianni", she said, drying her eyes.

Sanford looked at her and nodded.

"That's what I would have named you if... To me, you will always be Gianni."

In response to gentle probing by Sanford, more of the story came out. Joe sent Maria pictures of Sanford, but she had to be careful with them, and in the end she did find a safe place to hide them. Joe had told her about Aileen, and Maria admitted to sharp pangs of jealousy, until she realized that her son would be raised by someone who appeared to be as devoted to him as Maria was.

The years went by. Joe suggested to Aileen when Sanford was about twelve that they should tell him about his past. Aileen was aghast, terrified that Sanford would somehow lose his regard for the person he had considered his mother, that she, Aileen, could lose the most valuable thing in her life. She begged Joe not to say anything. So he didn't, and time moved on.

Later, Joe suggested again to Aileen, when Sanford was in his twenties, that they should tell him. But the old terror awoke again in Aileen, if anything in even greater strength. "He will react badly to being not told all these years", she said. She feared, again, that Sanford would turn against her, and she would lose him. So, they kept quiet.

Then, Aileen died suddenly.

"Joe kept saying he was going to tell you the whole story", Maria said. "He even said he had set a date to do that. I didn't know why he had suddenly changed his mind about telling you, but I think he was also afraid of you being angry."

Sanford's expression was frozen in place, and he gazed into the distance. Maria looked at him. "What's wrong?"

"That was why Joe wanted to see me", Sanford said, looking blindly past Maria. Maria's hand tightened on Sanford's arm, expressing an unspoken question. He turned to look at her. "Joe and I had agreed I would spend three or four days with him. I had already booked the time off work. He was probably going to tell me then."

A feeling of great wistfulness settled over Sanford.

"Joe died the Saturday before that."

"Oh Gianni! No! I'm sorry!"

At last, the ghosts from Sanford's past, ghosts that had risen only recently, were being laid to rest. Sanford took Maria's hand firmly in his, and nodded toward the bedroom door, from behind which they could now hear murmuring. "Your granddaughter is awake. It's time you met her."

Maria flushed visibly in expectant joy.

# Twenty-eight

When Sanford and Maria entered the bedroom, Julia was dressed, sitting on the bed, and brushing her hair.

"Hi Julia", Sanford said. "Come and meet Uncle Joe's friend Maria."

Sanford watched them both closely. Maria smiled brilliantly, and walked over to Julia holding out both hands. Julia was a little uncertain, but she moved toward Maria, took her hands, and a smile slowly formed on her face.

"*Ciao* Giulia", Maria said, and Sanford sensed immediately that, in her own mind, Maria saw the Italian spelling of Julia's name.

"*Ciao* Maria", Julia replied, since she had liked the word *ciao* as soon as Sanford had explained it to her.

Maria laughed softly, put her arm around Julia's shoulders, and they both turned to face Sanford.

"Did you know Uncle Joe well, Maria?"

"Yes. I knew him very well."

"He was as nice as Daddy."

Maria looked at Sanford mischievously. "Oh, I think he was nicer."

Sanford looked at both of them and grunted.

"Well", he began dubiously, "despite the insults, this is a special occasion and I think we need to celebrate." The suite had a small bar fridge, just big enough to accommodate a bottle of Prosecco once all the other bottles had been removed. Sanford lined up three glasses, took the Prosecco out of the fridge, and opened it. The pop of the cork made Julia giggle, and she couldn't wait for a small glass to be poured for her.

Sanford handed a full glass to Maria, a tasting portion to Julia, and raised his own glass.

"Let's drink to Uncle Joe and to us."

Sanford led them to the chairs near the window, they sat, and he and Maria both began answering questions from Julia, while carefully dodging the central truth. They talked for about half an hour, Julia moving her chair gradually closer to Maria's and smiling up at her.

Sanford divided the last of the wine among them, and said that they should think about going out somewhere for dinner.

"I'm getting hungry", Julia said.

But Maria was shaking her head.

"We will all go out for dinner, but to my place. I cook you something really special. What did you eat for lunch, Giulia?"

"I had pasta and some nice fishy things."

"Well, I have some nice things for dinner as well."

"You shouldn't have to cook for us, Maria", Sanford objected.

"For me cooking is a pleasure. You must come."

It was soon clear that nothing would budge her from this project, so Sanford relented. Having won that battle, Maria was eager to lay out a plan for how they would fill what was left of the day. "First, we look at Genoa." And look at Genoa they did.

Maria appeared to be versed in all the history of the city, and rhymed it off as they walked. But she kept it general, since Julia had had no schooling yet, and what she knew was limited to the few shreds she had picked up from Sanford. They walked along part of *Via San Luca* before diving off through a maze of *caruggi*, the charming little lanes that riddle the old city. They covered part of *Via Garibaldi* again, and when she heard the name *Garibaldi*, Julia exclaimed "Giuseppe!" Maria looked at Sanford in a mixture of astonishment and delight, and whispered "*Bravissimo!*" to him. They walked and walked. Julia seemed impossible to tire, and she was full of questions. The narrow twisting streets fascinated her, and she kept tugging at Maria's sleeve asking about this or that feature they were passing. Sanford tried to keep track of where he was for a while, but eventually admitted he hadn't a clue, and just tagged along. They rode the funicular to Mount Righi, and spent fifteen minutes just taking in the afternoon view, the sun slanting across the harbour and the breeze sweeping through palm fronds.

"Okay", Maria said decisively. "Time to go. We need to eat soon, and you can help me do the cooking, Giulia."

"What will Daddy do?"

"Daddy will look after the wine. Off we go!"

Within minutes they were in a taxi heading back once again to Boccadasse.

Not having had any real chance to take in the features of Boccadasse during the previous taxi ride, when he had picked up Maria, Sanford spent time looking around as the taxi made its way to Maria's building.

A unique piece of the exceptional Genoese quilt, Boccadasse is tucked in at the eastern end of the city. It has blocks of flats, some of them quite nice, set at invitingly irregular angles on the hills that climb out of the sea. Rows of upturned fishing and sailing boats line the upper end of a small and fairly scruffy bit of rough stony beach. There are little local bistros, a few shops, three reasonably broad streets snaking up the hillsides, and a warren of lanes conforming grumpily to the irregular framework dictated by the buildings. As they had approached Boccadasse, what Sanford came to recognize as the signature profile of the place – the elegant jumble of perched buildings – stood out against the flat background of the sea.

The building containing Maria's flat was a solid five-storey affair. Sanford paid the driver, and they all bundled into the building and up to Maria's flat. The flat was laid out in what would be known in

Toronto as a relatively spacious one-bedroom, having a generously large kitchen and living–dining room area. Maria watched Sanford look around in appraisal.

"I've lived here more than twenty-five years", she said, "and finished paying for this place about five years ago. A lot of the payments came from contributions from Joe."

"Joe sent you money?" Sanford asked, and then hesitated at his own unintended rudeness.

Maria smiled. "Every year. He also visited me here every year, and on each visit he had a building project."

"Does she mean Uncle Joe, Daddy?" Julia asked, looking at Sanford.

"Yes, Uncle Joe", Maria replied. "He was an amazing man. Did you know, Giulia, that he could speak Italian … what was that word … fluently, yes, fluently?"

Sanford remembered the annotated books he had found in Joe's spare room.

"After a couple of years, we wrote to each other only in Italian because his Italian had become much better than my English."

"But your English is excellent!" Sanford objected.

"That give you some idea how good was Joe's Italian. After a few years, he had friends here."

Maria showed them around her neat and colourfully decorated flat. Joe's hand was evident almost everywhere, from the tiling in the bathroom and kitchen, to the rich woods in Maria's bedroom, to the plaster and paint in the living area, to the bookcases. Everything was done matching a local style, but the flat sheen on the wood surfaces, the whimsically appealing tiling patterns, and the careful imperfections incorporated into the plastering and painting might as well have borne Joe's physical signature.

"How long would he stay, when he came here?" Sanford asked.

"Never longer than two weeks, sometimes only a week or ten days."

Maria looked wistfully into a past that was evidently warm but also filled by *if onlys*.

"Did you travel much in Italy when Joe came to visit?" Sanford asked.

"No. We almost always stayed here. But Joe became very fond of Genoa. And he got to know Boccadasse well. He found the local book shop during his first visit, and quickly became friends with Franco, who owns it. Franco introduced Joe to a few other people, but the most important was Silvio, who is a policeman at the local detachment, but also collects work by poets who lived or still live near Lake Garda. In fact, all three of us once spent a weekend there, and Silvio showed Joe around Gabriele D'Annunzio's villa, *Il Vittoriale*, at Gardone Riviera. We spent most of a day there, and near the end of that day Silvio gave Joe a little something to remember the visit. It was a book called *Season of Storms*. Joe was surprised to find that it was in English, and even more surprised when Silvio told him that it was written by one of Joe's compatriots. Ever since that visit, Silvio always checks to make sure that I'm all right, that I have everything I need. Silvio and Joe had become good friends."

Here, Maria drifted into another short reminiscence.

"Joe never stayed long enough during those visits", she said softly. "He always said he had … responsibilities … to go back to", and she rubbed an eyebrow in a vain attempt to hide tears that had leaked out.

"Are you okay, Maria?" Julia asked in obvious concern.

"Oh, yes, Giulia dear, I'm fine. Just a bit tired and hungry. So, come! Both of you! Into the kitchen! We start dinner."

Sanford realized that they had spent quite some time looking around Maria's flat and talking, and dusk had settled outside. Maria began pulling things from her small fridge, from her oven, and from cupboards.

"So, we have some nice focaccia, which I warm up now, and olive oil, good local olive oil, and some olives, then we have pasta with a *salsa di noci*", and here she looked to Sanford who managed to supply a translation – "walnut sauce" – "then we have chicken, how you say *farcito* … ah yes, stuffed, stuffed by pesto and cheese, and then we have some nice lemon cake and fruit."

"*Gianni! Vino! Nel frigo, per favore.* Giulia, please take these olives and olive oil to the table, then come back for knives and forks. *Gianni! I bicchiere sono nel armadietto a destra.*" It took Sanford a couple of seconds to decode all this – the wine being in the fridge, and glasses in the right-hand cupboard. By the time Sanford and Julia had completed their tasks, Maria had the elements for the entire meal laid out. Water was on for cooking the pasta, and a plate of focaccia was warming in the oven.

The wine was poured, a very pleasant white from Cinque Terre, and Maria raised her glass, saying with obvious pride and generous hospitality "Welcome to my home, my dear friends."

Julia moved to a bookcase to the left of the window, and began examining the hundred or so books neatly ranged so that their spines all sat on a common line about an inch in from the edges of the shelves.

Maria watched Julia closely. "Do you read, Giulia?"

"Yes", Julia said somewhat absently as she continued her perusal.

Maria looked at Sanford and raised an eyebrow. "Yes. I've taught her to read over the past couple of years ... when I was allowed to visit or have her at my place ... but we've done a lot more over the past few weeks."

Julia ran her finger along the books. "The words are funny", she said in disappointment, but then smiled brightly.

"Pinocchio!"

She drew the book from the shelf, opened it, and then her smile collapsed once more.

"Let me read you a bit of it", Maria said, and she began reading in slow, clear, lilting Italian. Sanford looked at Julia. Although she didn't understand a word, the beauty and the cadence of the language clearly was not lost on her.

Maria stopped reading near the end of the first page.

"Is that the same Pinocchio?" Julia asked.

"Yes, but in my language", Maria said through a small proud smile.

While Julia and Maria looked at Maria's copy of *Pinocchio*, Sanford had moved to the bookcase, and was scanning the titles.

There were Italian classics he recognized, particularly by Manzoni, Nievo, di Lampedusa, but he was surprised at the number of what appeared to be children's books. *Mi piace il cioccolato* by Davide Calì, *Il piccolo Alpino* by Salvator Gotta, *Il romanzo di Cipollino* by Gianni Rodari. Sanford looked across at Maria, who was paging through *Pinocchio* with Julia.

"I like that", Julia said, a strangely serious expression on her face. "Could I learn that too?"

"Of course you could", Maria said.

"Would you like to learn Italian, Julia?" Sanford asked.

"Mmmm", Julia said, nodding.

Children's books. Their mere presence here in Maria's flat spoke poignant volumes, and Sanford realized suddenly how much catching up there was to do, how much Julia had to learn about the three extraordinary people in Sanford's past – and necessarily in her past as well – and how much Maria had to learn about Sanford's past. Joe would have told her quite a bit, but there was a lot that not even Joe had known. There was also a rich future, to be crammed into the time left to Maria, and that future involved the three of them. It all seemed now to Sanford so clear and so urgent and so important.

"Excellent! Then I teach you Italian, Giulia", Maria said. "But not before we have dinner! Please, sit. The focaccia will be warm. I go and get it."

And so they began a long, relaxed, delicious meal. Maria retreated to the kitchen at strategically chosen times, so that the passage from course to course was leisurely but seamless. Julia had never had olives or focaccia before, and had never had fresh olive oil, and her expressions reflected what were to her new and exotic tastes. Pasta with a walnut sauce followed, and this was new to Sanford as well. Maria had prepared the stuffed chicken herself, and had made the pesto as well, and Sanford exclaimed involuntarily at the first bite.

"This really is delicious, Maria. It looks simple as well, but I'm sure it's not."

"No! It really is easy, Gianni. Tomorrow we go and buy you a book of *ricette italiane*."

The last of the wine was poured, they finished the chicken course at a stately pace, and Sanford opened a bottle of sweeter wine in preparation for the dessert.

Maria carried in a handsome-looking lemon cake and a bowl of fresh figs, pears, and apricots.

"Maria! This is fantastic! Look at the colours, Julia!" Sanford exclaimed, but Julia needed no prompting.

Maria was about to sit down again when there was a knock at the door. She cast a puzzled expression at Sanford, glanced toward the clock on the wall, and rose to see who it could be.

"*Sì?*" Maria began as she opened the door a crack, but then the door flew open violently, and she was pushed back into the room.

Behind her, standing in the doorway, was a man whose face Sanford recognized. It was the face of a man who had been dead for almost a month.

# Twenty-nine

It took a few seconds for Sanford's mind to begin working again, and the trigger for that was Julia moving behind him and grabbing his arm. He didn't need to see her face to know that she was terrified.

Maria was the first to respond.

"*Chi sei? Che cosa vuoi?*" she demanded.

"Cut the babble lady", the intruder barked. "My business is with him", and he nodded at Sanford.

"This is my house", Maria screamed. "You can't just –", but she was cut off by a blow across the face, using whatever it was the intruder held in his hand, causing her to stumble and fall in the doorway to the kitchen.

Sanford began to rise, but the intruder said "Stay where you are Sanford", while waving his arm, and making it clear that what he held in the hand doing the waving was a pistol, a pistol that had a long silencer. Sanford sat back down slowly.

Cold, dark fear gripped him. But the fear was for Julia's safety, and it was fear like he had never known before.

"That's better", said the intruder. "You probably didn't expect to see me, did you?"

"It's not a question of expecting to see you or anybody", Sanford said quietly after a short delay. "I have no idea who you are."

"Oh, yes! Go ahead, then. Play the innocent if you want. And it's just possible that you don't know me, although I doubt that very much. I'm David Jeffers, my brother is Charles, the man that bastard Joe Stanton probably killed."

Sanford sat there, mute.

Jeffers stood glaring at Sanford, and nodding in an odd and vacant way. "Charles and me had a good thing", he said, at last. "But I haven't seen him or heard from him for almost a month, and he would never do that. Unless he was dead. And that's very likely the case. And it could only have been Joe Stanton."

Jeffers hesitated. He said, not looking at anyone in particular "We had a very good thing. Charles was the brains, but we're identical twins." A pause here. "I really don't exist – no driver's licence, no cards, no government ID, no property, no income. So I could easily alibi Charles whenever he needed it. It was almost impossible for the police to make anything stick, because we were always careful. We never went anywhere together. And nobody could ever tell one of us from the other."

The look in Jeffers' face was strange – distant, disconnected, confused, angry. It occurred to Sanford that Jeffers was close to being unhinged. His pistol hand waved about slowly, ominously, like a cornered snake, and Sanford realized that he was facing a threat that was real, barely rational, and exceptionally dangerous. *Don't do anything to tip him over the edge. Get Julia someplace safe. How? Clamp down on the rising panic. Think! Think! Think!!*

Jeffers suddenly refocused, looking directly at Sanford. "But that's all gone, and now I want what's mine. Your old man, Harold Sanford, screwed us royally, a real first-rate bastard, he cleaned out all the money we had worked together with him to get, and then he pinched a lot of stuff that was ours as well, stuff he had no claim on. Now I want it back. And you're going to tell me where I can find him."

Sanford shook his head. "I haven't spoken to Harold Sanford for more than thirty years. I have no idea where he is. Or even whether he's still alive."

"Nice try, Sanford. But I know that he shifted a large sum of money to you recently. Probably told you it was saved from his sales income. Hah! Just so much bullshit! It was syphoned from me and Charles, that's where it came from! And he still has more! Lots more! So, if I was you, I would decide to tell me what I want to know, and I'd start talking soon."

"I don't know what to say", Sanford began. "I have no connection to Harold –"

"That's the way you want it?" Jeffers shouted, waving the pistol in agitation. "Okay! Maybe if I do a little work on your daughter you might change your mind!"

Jeffers began moving toward them, and Sanford's blood froze. He reached out and pushed Julia gently so that she was further behind him. Sanford tried to keep his facial expression neutral, and he began to rise slowly as Jeffers approached. Jeffers' expression was crazed. His eyes were wide and they burnt brightly, a conduit to the outside for some ferocious inner fire. Sanford looked into a personal abyss as it became clear that there was no way he would ever convince Jeffers that he had absolutely zero information on Harold, and realized, as a result, that if Jeffers got his hands on Julia, there would be nothing Sanford could say that would get her back. Other thoughts rushed through Sanford's brain, but one that he recalled vividly later was the question *Why would Jeffers come all the way to Italy to confront me and what possible workable plan might he have in mind?* All at once, it became blindingly clear to Sanford: Jeffers had nothing one could call a plan. No longer having a rock-solid brother to lean on, he wanted some kind of revenge, wanted to be freed from his present intolerable situation, wanted to be able to hide behind a pile of cash, wanted Sanford to wave a magic wand and make it all go away. Jeffers was indeed mad.

The only weapon in front of Sanford was the table and what lay on it, virtually useless, since Jeffers could fire two shots in less than a second, and Sanford, or worse, Julia, would be history. What to do? How could he possibly protect Julia? He had nothing to tell Jeffers, no knowledge whatsoever of Harold, so Julia was in extreme danger. In fact, when it came right to the wire, they were all in extreme danger, and it was probable that Jeffers would kill them all. So, a heroic measure might be the only option open. Sanford's logic was barely afloat on a heaving sea of panic and despair. What to do? What to do?

A movement just caught Sanford's eye. Suddenly there was a loud clang, and Jeffers leapt sideways, falling in a heap on the floor. His pistol clattered on the tiles and skidded down the hallway. Maria's face had a long, open cut down the left cheek, and she was holding the large black skillet she had used to strike Jeffers on the side of the head. Jeffers moaned, and Maria made to move toward him.

"No! Maria! We have to get Julia out of here!" Suddenly energized, but still deathly afraid, he grabbed a petrified Julia, took Maria by one arm, and rushed toward the door. Maria halted briefly, dropped the skillet, grabbed a cellphone from the small table next to the door, and then they were running down the hallway. Behind them there was a loud roar, Jeffers voicing the anger of a wounded animal. Julia tripped and began to sob. Maria was jabbing desperately at her phone, but Sanford was focused on picking up Julia and getting to the end of the hall, where there was a door that appeared to be an exit.

"Sanford!" Jeffers roared from within Maria's flat. Maria now was speaking into her phone in rapid Italian. All Sanford could pick out was "*Ha una pistola! O mio Dio Silvio! Fa' presto! Fa' presto!*" but then the phone slipped from her hands. She looked down at it, and began stooping to pick it up, but Sanford grabbed her roughly.

"Leave it Maria! Go! Go!"

"Sanford! You bastard!" Jeffers roared again.

The end of the hallway was like a faint galaxy: distant and receding. Maria was now running, although she appeared to stagger occasionally, probably still woozy from being struck. Sanford tried to reach out and support her, but doing so made them bump together and jostle one another, causing them to bounce lightly off the walls, slowing them down. He kept saying to Maria "Go! Go! Faster! Faster! He's right behind us!" Maria did everything she could to slide her hands along the walls, support herself, maintain balance, and continue running. Julia was sobbing now, terrified out of her wits, and Sanford realized that she was running almost alongside him, a target if Jeffers came into the hallway and began firing. Sanford pushed Julia in front of himself. "Grab Maria's dress!" he said to Julia, as calmly as he could, but he felt that despite his effort it still came out as an eldritch screech.

They were almost at the door now.

"Sanford! You've just made this a lot worse for yourself!" The change in his voice told Sanford he was now at least partly in the hallway. Maria slammed into the door, it opened, and she and Julia were through into a stairwell.

It was then that Jeffers fired.

*Phht! Phht!*

A piece of the door flew away, and Sanford was showered by wood splinters, but then he too was in the stairwell. "Down! Down!" he shouted, but Maria was already descending as fast as she could, almost tripping at every step, and dragging Julia behind her. Another roar of rage from Jeffers was cut off as the door closed slowly behind them.

One flight down. Then another half flight.

"Sanford!"

Jeffers was now in the stairwell.

They continued stumbling down the stairs, Julia was sobbing continuously, Maria was muttering something to herself. Sanford tried to look ahead, to see where the exit was from the building, but his view was cut off by the tight corners in the narrow stairwell.

Sanford could hear Jeffers stumbling down behind them. He had no idea how far they were ahead of him, and prayed that Jeffers' line of sight down the stairs to them was as obscured as his was of the exit somewhere below.

*Phht!*

The bullet struck the wall ahead of and above them. Chunks of plaster and construction block pattered down the stairs, and bounced off Maria and Julia. Julia wailed loudly.

"Keep going!" Sanford shouted ahead to them. "I'm right behind you!"

And then, there it was, less than one more flight down. The exit from the building. Jeffers was stumbling behind and above them, and Sanford choked off the fear that he was catching up to them, by focusing on that exit door. Somewhere outside, the distinctive tones of an emergency vehicle were rising in the distance. *Please God, let it be the police*, Sanford said fervently to himself.

There was a clatter behind them in the stairwell, and a lot of loud cursing from Jeffers.

"Sanford! You bastard! You've had it now!"

They crashed through the exit door and into the night. Maria collided with a large waste bin, and would have fallen had Sanford not grabbed her by the arm and hauled her back up fully to her feet. Julia was sobbing in panic, but Sanford's other hand had her arm in an iron grip, despite the fact that he seemed strangely to have lost feeling in that hand. He looked around frantically. To their right was just an obscure darkness that could have concealed anything, including a dead end. To the left was open space, but at least a car was parked there.

"This way!" he shouted, and dragged them both forcibly toward the car. The emergency vehicle was very near now. The three of them rounded the front of the car.

"Sanford!" Jeffers roared. He was now out in the night with them.

Out of what he later realized must have been pure instinct, Sanford dived behind the car, dragging Maria and Julia with him. They all struck the ground heavily.

*Phht! Phht!*

Two windows in the car suddenly crazed. Splinters of glass showered down onto them.

Headlight beams swung past, illuminating the car they were sheltering behind and reflecting off the windows of nearby buildings.

"Sanford!"

Then a challenge was shouted in Italian.

*Phht! Phht!*

There was a groan and the sound of metal striking stone.

Four loud rapid-fire barks from a service Beretta reverberated around the closed space among the buildings. Then silence, apart from the sounds of Maria and Julia weeping as they lay on the ground.

"*Maria? Dove sei? Sono Silvio.*" There was more rapid Italian, sounding like Silvio speaking into a cellphone.

Silvio said something else rapidly and they heard a faint murmur in reply. Someone began walking in their direction.

"Maria?" Silvio's voice was very close now. And then he was rushing toward them, the word *Polizia* clearly visible across the front of his vest.

He knelt by Maria, spoke to her softly, and then helped her to her feet.

"*L'intruso*?" she asked, in a quavery voice.

"*Morto*", Silvio answered.

Sanford got to his feet, pulling Julia up, but she clutched at Sanford ferociously. In what Sanford saw as a response to the extreme stress of the situation, Julia struggled to say something through spasmodic sobs.

"Da-Daddy. You, you're not going to d-die, are you?" Sanford looked at her and realized she was wide-eyed, but not focusing on his face. It was then he saw that his left hand, his entire left arm was covered in blood, and that there was a large flap of skin hanging just below his shoulder. One of Jeffers' shots as they were entering the stairwell must have grazed his arm.

Another emergency vehicle was sounding through the night, quickly coming closer. Silvio said something more to Maria. "*Sì*", she answered, and Silvio moved away as an ambulance came to a stop next to the police car.

The lights from the ambulance flickered around the space enclosed by the nearby buildings. Faces had appeared at windows, and there was muffled conversation. Another police car pulled in, just as the ambulance was leaving. Sanford leaned against the car they had sheltered behind, and he was now shaking from shock. He picked up a sobbing Julia, held her to his chest, and felt her tears trickle down his neck. Even years later, that image stayed with him.

Sanford had suffered just a light flesh wound, but it looked far worse than it was. Silvio's partner had been first out of the police car, even before it had stopped, and although both Jeffers' shots had hit him, the wounds turned out not to be a threat to his life. The ambulance had come at Silvio's request to rush his partner to the hospital. Silvio was known as a crack shot at the police firing range, and all four of his shots had struck Jeffers in the chest. Most likely, Jeffers was unconscious before he hit the ground, and dead only moments later.

Using the first-aid kit in his squad car, Silvio put a temporary binding on the wound on Sanford's shoulder until it could be treated properly by a doctor. A second ambulance arrived, but when the attendants had determined that Jeffers was dead, they waited until the necessary forensic work had been completed before loading the body in the ambulance and driving off. By eleven o'clock, the two police officers from the second car had taken statements from Maria, Sanford, and Silvio, and had shot what seemed to be hundreds of photos of the scene. By midnight, Sanford had left the hospital along with Maria and Julia, Sanford's shoulder having been stitched and properly bandaged, and Maria's face bandaged.

Silvio told Maria that she couldn't stay at her place since the investigators might be working inside for some time, and Sanford suggested that they all go to his hotel. Silvio dropped the three of them there and then left, but not before asking Maria at least four times if she was all right. He said that because he had shot someone, there would be a formal review, and he would spend the day at police headquarters in central Genoa.

The night clerk found a room for Maria, but they all went to Sanford and Julia's suite first. They sat together on the sofa, Julia between Maria and Sanford, sleep being no possibility for any of them despite their exhaustion.

"I think we need something", Sanford said. He rose a bit shakily, and went to the mini-bar. There were three small bottles of good grappa, and Sanford scooped them out, poured two of them into two glasses, and a smaller amount into a third glass, which he then diluted using mineral water.

"We should be drinking to something", Maria said vaguely, as she cupped the glass in her hands.

"Yes", Sanford said. "Let's drink to Silvio. *Un brindisi a Silvio! Il nostro salvatore!*"

Maria brightened immediately. "Yes. To Silvio!"

Even Julia managed a wan smile. "Silvio!"

# Thirty

The next morning Sanford awoke before the sun did.

He was a mass of conflicting feelings.

The violence of the night before immediately forced itself into his awareness, and sent a cold wave up his back. Raising a hand to run through his hair, he was surprised at the slight tremor he saw in it. A crowd of mixed images, both welcome and ghastly, skirmished at the edges of his consciousness, and the thought occurred that all this would take time to dissipate. Ignoring this confusion as best he could, Sanford turned to thoughts of the present and the future.

Through the bedroom window, a pinkish blue sky offered its invitation to the day. In the bed next to his, Julia lay sound asleep. Without warning, another image, one of Maria's face, completely unknown to him just twenty-four hours ago, swam before his eyes again, and he smiled involuntarily. But then a vision of Joe appeared, followed by a black presence that reached out effortlessly and against his every wish, across thousands of kilometres from a sordid, shallow grave. Forcing all this from his mind, if only temporarily, he tried to focus on the small number of clear objectives that now had prominence in his life.

The events of the night before kept replaying themselves in an endless loop, although he thought their impact was fading as he tried to orient himself to the day. There were some practical things to be done. He would let Conway know later that day just what had happened, asking him to keep his ear to the ground for any reaction in Canada. As far as anyone but Sanford was concerned, the man who had attempted to kill them was Charles Jeffers. Sanford would probe gently, later, to determine whether Maria had heard anything Jeffers had said about himself and his brother, and whether she remembered any of it. She was the only other adult in a position to know that anybody called David Jeffers had even existed.

In his mind, Sanford tied up some loose ends concerning the Jeffers brothers. David Jeffers appeared to have spent his life becoming and remaining a ghost, as a means of having Charles Jeffers be in two places at the same time whenever the need for that arose, and in the end that had worked against him. Had he lived, probably he would have re-emerged at some point as his brother. But he must have known that there was a large gap between his and his brother's mental capabilities and that somebody would have noticed that difference very soon after his reappearance as "Charles". Once that happened, there would have been trouble of various sorts awaiting him. But the shooting of "Charles Jeffers" in Boccadasse had cut off the future right there for both Jeffers. David Jeffers had presumably travelled to Italy using Charles's passport, and that document would be shipped back to Canada along with the body. Almost certainly, the presence of Jeffers and Sanford in Italy at the same time would be noticed by various underworld figures in Canada, and by the police, since Sanford had made no particular secret of his travel plans. The police in Canada would surely investigate, but it seemed clear to Sanford that they would get nowhere. Sanford himself could expect to be interviewed. The investigation would stall and the case would be closed.

From what turned out to be David Jeffers' last speech in Maria's apartment, he had guessed what had happened to his brother. But he was stymied, he could do nothing about it. He could hardly approach the police, even indirectly, claiming that Charles Jeffers had been murdered, because as far as all the rest of the world was concerned, he *was* Charles Jeffers.

Without much doubt, Harold would be among the first to know back in Canada about what had happened, given that he seemed to be well connected. That Charles Jeffers was killed in a shoot-out in Genoa while apparently attempting to kill Sanford probably would be a surprise to Harold, but a welcome surprise. From Harold's point of view, the last significant finger that could point to him now had been cut off. Harold would be free of any future threat from Jeffers.

There were uncertainties ahead for Sanford, but he hoped that his assessment of them as "second order" would turn out to be correct. Further probing by Conway, having Conway listen to the underworld chatter, a closed police investigation, and, in time, the decline of the whole matter into obscurity was what Sanford hoped for. He hoped that he, Julia, and Maria would see an unobstructed future. The three of them had a great deal to do, and the considerable literary estate and financial resource Joe had left behind would figure prominently in all that.

And then there was Joe.

Dear, wonderful, Joe. Oh, Joe! Why did it all have to work out just this way? Joe had killed Charles Jeffers, and Sanford was now convinced that he had done that to protect Sanford and Julia. Joe had seen what one version of the future might have been, and he took steps to pinch off that future. Oh, Joe! A lot of that must remain our secret, yours and mine, but if you are out there anywhere Joe, if you can see and hear us, you have one eternally grateful friend, and one humbly admiring son.

Sanford rose, showered, and shaved. Before climbing into the shower, he had pulled off the dressing on his shoulder wound. The wound looked purple and angry, but there were signs it was already beginning to heal. He then showered as carefully as possible, replaced the dressing using the package he had been given at the hospital, and then selected shorts and a loose-fitting golf shirt for the day. Blue shorts. Of course.

Sanford had succumbed this trip, and brought an iPad as well as his cellphone, and he set to work on both of those.

First, he sent an email to Conway, attaching two photos, and asked Conway to dig up as much information as possible on the younger man in the second of the two attached photos. He requested that Conway get back to him as soon as possible when he had anything that looked important, reminding Conway that he was in Europe so not to bother trying to phone.

Second, he sent an email to Silvio, in the best Italian he could manage, but leaning heavily on his dictionary, and repeating the message in English in case he had turned the Italian completely into cabbage. He offered a simple and heartfelt thanks to Silvio, and then asked Silvio for any details that could be provided on the intruder to Maria's flat – particularly when and where he had arrived in Italy and whether he was working alone – and also asked Silvio when and where he should turn up with Maria to finish any paperwork connected to the events of the previous evening.

Third, he sent an email to Inspector Meloni, telling him that he and Julia were out of the country, asking if there was any further information the police could share on the man in whose apartment Sanford's ex-wife had been, asking if he would mind checking on Helen's parents, whose address and names he also provided to Meloni, and thanking him and Sergeant Howell for the care and attention they had given the case.

Sanford then called to Maria's room to check that she was okay, to tell her about his communication to Silvio and the probable need later that morning to finish off some paperwork with the police, but most importantly to arrange a time for the three of them to have breakfast. Maria was fine but groggy, probably had not had a good sleep, and said that she would come to Sanford's suite in about forty-five minutes.

"Daddy?" Sanford was aware immediately of the concern conveyed by the sleepy voice from the bedroom.

"Yes. I'm here", and he went immediately into the bedroom.

Julia was examining, in some alarm, a large bloodstain on the sheets.

"It's okay. My bandage just wept a bit in the night. I'm fine. Did you sleep okay?"

"Yes."

"No nightmares?"

"No. That man won't come back, will he?"

"No Julia, he won't be coming back."

"Good. I don't want him to hurt you."

Sanford smiled and swallowed the lump in his throat. "Would you like a shower?" he managed to croak.

"Yes."

"And then some breakfast with Maria?"

"Oh! Yes, please."

Seeing Sanford move around without effort or pain caused Julia's concern to fade, and she climbed out of bed and headed to the bathroom. Sanford returned to his iPad.

Silvio had replied to Sanford's email. Sanford was not surprised to learn that there were no details on the intruder. He jotted down the address of the police station in central Genoa, where he and Maria could turn up any time during the morning to finish off the last paperwork details on the previous night's events.

Sanford was very surprised, however, to see a reply from Conway, since it was the wee hours of the morning in Toronto. Conway's message was just an acknowledgement of Sanford's email and a statement that Conway would be working on his request starting almost immediately. Insomniac? Sanford shrugged and emailed back his thanks to Conway.

Sanford could hear that Julia had just finished in the shower, and he sat, pondering things idly. Julia soon appeared, proudly wearing another pair of her blue shorts. She walked across the room and leaned against Sanford.

Maria arrived in their suite, dressed, out of necessity, in the same clothes she had worn the day before, a bit puffy-eyed, but smiling and ready for the day. Julia went immediately to Maria and gave her a long spontaneous hug. This prompted a smiling three-party "good morning", and then they all set off.

The brilliant Italian sunshine slammed into their faces, nudging them into generous squinty smiles and a shared feeling of well-being. Bare arms and legs were tickled by the morning breeze, which also tugged capriciously at wisps of hair. Maria knew a good spot for breakfast, and soon they were settled around an assortment of bread, fruit, cheese, orange juice, and coffee.

"What would you like to do today, Giulia?" Maria asked past a mouthful of bread.

"See more little streets."

Maria nodded.

"Have some spaghetti."

More nodding.

"Do some shopping."

At this Maria brightened, plucked at her dress, and said that she wanted to shop as well, buy something a little cooler, because she hadn't been thinking straight enough last night to ask the police if she could get a change of clothes from her flat.

Sanford had the clear impression that a primary activity for the day had just been decided, and that any opinion he might have had on the matter didn't need expressing, since it would have been superfluous no matter what it was. The three of them munched slowly through breakfast, and their periodic exchanges of smiles conveyed more meaning and more quiet delight than ever could have been delivered by words.

Sanford paid for breakfast. "*Allora. Andiamo!*" he pronounced, rising, and leaving it to Maria to deal with Julia's look of interested puzzlement at what Sanford had just said.

Sanford showed Maria the address Silvio had given him, Maria knew immediately where it was, and they walked the short distance there. The formalities were brief, and they were finished in twenty minutes. Maria and Silvio had a short rapid exchange, which Sanford later discovered was about Maria's cellphone and handbag, and he remembered her having dropped the cellphone in the hallway of her building. Silvio pulled a plastic bag from a shelf behind him and handed it to Maria, explaining that the investigators had found and bagged the cellphone, and he had asked them to retrieve her handbag as well, both of which were in the bag. There was another rapid exchange between Maria and Silvio. Maria explained later that the formal police review of the shooting would be completed by mid-afternoon, and that Silvio would see them in Boccadasse. Maria and Sanford said their *thank-yous* and *ciaos* to Silvio, and then the three of them were outside again.

They wandered once more, through the lovely main streets of Genoa, and Maria pointed out all the grand buildings constructed from the rivers of wealth that had flowed into Genoa during its long and storied past. She spoke about Nino Bixio, a tough-minded lieutenant among Garibaldi's famous thousand, and how that thousand had set out for Sicily from Quarto, a place not far from where Maria lived. Maria spoke about Albaro, also not far from where she lived, and that Charles Dickens (or Carlo Dickens, as the historical plaque reads at *Villa di Bella Vista*) had lived there briefly. She spoke about some familiar figures, Andrea Doria, Cristoforo Colombo, Giovanni Caboto, and about others Sanford had not heard of. This was all beyond Julia, but she paid rapt attention nonetheless, and both Maria and Sanford said that they would explain everything to her.

Maria met several of her friends in the street, stopped to talk to them, introduced Sanford and his daughter, and it was clear to Sanford that Maria was dying to say that "Giulia" was her granddaughter. One of the ladies they met flashed Julia a smile and asked her very slowly "*Come stai?*" When Julia replied "*Sto bene, grazie*" almost immediately, the smile became a little cry of delight and won Julia a hug.

Maria turned to Sanford. "Oh Gianni! She's learning Italian just like Joe did, so easily, so quickly!"

"She's young", Sanford replied. "Her mind is a sponge."

"Just like you. Joe always said that you learned quickly too."

"Yes", Sanford remarked sardonically. "My mind is also a sponge, but while her mind soaks up things, mine lets them leak out."

Maria squeezed Sanford's hand secretly, tightly, and the look on her face caused a warm feeling, long unfamiliar, to flood through him. One of his objectives would soon be within reach.

They walked on until suddenly Julia said loudly "Maria!", and pointed to women's shorts on display in a shop window. Maria and Julia vanished abruptly into the shop, reminding Sanford of comments he had heard about things being sucked into black holes. Standing abandoned in the street, Sanford reminded himself pedantically that black holes don't suck.

Twenty minutes later, Maria reappeared through the event horizon wearing a dashing pair of new shorts (blue, of course) and a loose and comfortable-looking pink top. Julia was right behind her, wearing a new pair of shorts in the Italian national colours and a pink top that matched Maria's. They looked at each other and giggled enthusiastically.

"Daddy, you should buy something", Julia said when the giggling had died down.

"Nonsense! I'd look really silly in a pink top."

"Noo-oo! I didn't mean that!", and then the giggling began anew.

They walked some more. They talked much more. Eventually, at almost one o'clock, Sanford said they should find someplace to have some lunch.

"I already have a place", Maria said. "Follow me."

She led them to another of the funicular railways, and they rode it to the top. Five minutes later, they were seated at a small hilltop bistro that had a stunning view out over Genoa harbour. The aquamarine Ligurian Sea stretched languidly off to the south. The city's buildings, a fascinating jumble of forms and colours, set wherever there was space on the folded hills, were visual poetry. Looking across at Julia, Sanford saw a young girl placed suddenly in a new and overwhelming context, and concentrating fiercely to memorize everything.

"Do you remember *The Recipe Cops*, Gianni?"

Those words, coming from Maria, caught him very much by surprise.

"Yes, of course. That was our little hideaway in the pines, Joe's and mine. Why did you remember that? *How* did you remember that?"

Maria smiled.

"Do you remember how you named it that?" she asked.

"Yes", Sanford said, somewhat puzzled. "But it was just a name that Joe picked. It doesn't mean anything." The words were scarcely out of his mouth when Sanford sensed, without really knowing why, that he had just uttered a strange statement. As a young boy, way back then, he had heard and understood the word "Cops", since it meant something to him and he was then unaware of the term "copse". Not until many years later, he realized that Joe actually had said "copse", but by then the place really had become *The Recipe Cops*, even though the term had no literal meaning.

Maria was shaking her head. "It wasn't just any name. When Joe was here, or I mean when we were in Rome, his favourite piece of music was *The Pines of Rome*. He played it all the time. I got tired of it, but he never did. Much later, when he visited me in Genoa, he told me that he played it for you many times in Canada as well. And he said to me, too many times to count, that the pines near his house always reminded him of Rome, even though those pines and the pines in Rome are very different."

She halted there briefly, reminiscing.

"He told me that the two of you were listening to his record of *The Pines of Rome* one day before lunch, and when the piece finished, you said 'I'm hungry, Joe', so he said you took some lunch out to what Joe called your special place. That was the day you picked a name for the place, Joe had already started to think about it as Respighi's Copse, he suggested some names for your little secret place, and that was one of them. Right away, you called it *The Recipe Cops*, not knowing who or what 'Respighi' was, and that's what it was from then on. Joe was so pleased about that. He told me the story every time he was here."

Sanford was dumbfounded. He realized that their special spot had always been The Recipe Cops for him. He had never questioned where the name came from. Having Maria's account of how it had got its name made the place ten times as important for him. Even though Joe knew what was behind the name The Recipe Cops, he had never discussed it with Sanford, and he knew why now. Explaining it, examining it, analysing it, would have been like revealing to a child that her favourite fairy tale was a load of crap. Joe had kept intact the name The Recipe Cops, a term that was meaningless in any ordinary semantic sense, but was still full of mystical significance for Sanford. It was then, and in some ways was even more now, a little mystery, a little piece of magic.

For what seemed a long time, Sanford sat in a reverie, listening to the sounds of Genoa all around him.

God bless you Joe.

Suddenly back in the present, Sanford suggested that they pay for lunch and take a taxi back to the hotel. A few words from Maria to the waiter organized that. Within twenty minutes, they were back in Sanford's suite. He expected Julia to be fatigued, but the surroundings and the companionship of the day had shifted her into adrenaline overdrive.

Maria began making noises about going home, and Julia's face fell.

"But aren't you at home here Maria?" she asked somewhat plaintively.

"I feel completely at home here Giulia, but I have my house to look after."

Julia almost did a pout, but then her face cleared. "Could I come and stay with you Maria?"

Maria turned to Sanford, and he could see a bright inner light burning behind her eyes.

"I don't see why not", he said.

"Are you coming too, Daddy?"

"No, I don't think so. I'll just come over during the day. How's that?"

"Okay. Can I take my new suitcase?"

"I think you'll need to take it. You can't carry your clothes in a plastic bag. So, maybe Maria can go and help make sure you have everything you need." He had barely finished the statement when they were bustling off to the bedroom.

Sanford's mind returned to the emails he had sent earlier. Genoa so far had been like a sweet dream of discovery, marked by a single nightmare episode that Sanford knew would fade quickly for all of them. In comparison to what he expected from the next two weeks, even just thinking about the realities that would be waiting for him back in Toronto was unwelcome. But he tipped all that over the side in order to tune in to the happy chatter trickling out from the bedroom.

A ping from Sanford's iPad indicated another incoming email. Surely it couldn't be Meloni at this time of his night.

It wasn't.

*Dear Jim,*

*You might have heard already, or you will soon hear, about the fate that befell a slimy little bastard called Lulu. I think that is the last loose end tied off. This saves you the trouble and risk of going after the little prick yourself. Call it my last parting gift. Enjoy your life. You won't hear from me again. Don't try to contact me. You won't find me.*

*Harold.*

Sanford was mystified. He really had no idea what Harold was talking about. He sat there puzzling over the words for a few minutes, then gave up.

He was about to write a quick friendly note to Maxwell, just to keep in touch, when his iPad pinged a second time. It was another email from Conway. When Sanford opened it, he was surprised at how long the email was.

Conway related a number of details. There was a lot of chatter in the underworld, he said. Even though the picture Sanford had sent was not great quality, being a picture taken of a picture, Conway had had no trouble finding people who could identify the two men. (Apparently,

Conway's world never slept.) The older one was Charles Jeffers, which was what had attracted Sanford's eye to the photo of two men he had spotted when he was in the apartment with Howell, where Helen's cellphone had been found. While Howell had been busy making notes, Sanford had used his phone to take an image of the framed picture. Conway's reply indicated that the younger man in the picture went by several names, but the nickname everyone knew him by was "Lulu". Lulu was one of Jeffers' gophers. The two of them apparently did small jobs together, but Lulu undertook any shit work that Jeffers wanted done.

This information had Sanford reeling already, but the real kicker was the last three sentences in Conway's email: *Lulu was found yesterday morning in a cheap hotel off Dundas Street West in Toronto. He was lying naked on the bed and had been strangled manually. More details when I can get them.*

Sanford sat in stunned silence for at least a minute.

"Holy Christ", he muttered to himself, feeling a tsunami of anger, hatred, and revulsion begin to overwhelm him. Helen's death hadn't been what he reluctantly had come to suspect, kinky sex gone wrong! More likely, Lulu had tried to throttle information out of Helen and went too far! Or maybe he got something from her and thought it was what he wanted. Or maybe, having unmasked himself, he just finished Helen off, eliminated a source of incrimination, just another task in a busy day. Sanford was breathing heavily, and realized that his fists were clenched so tightly that one of his fingernails had pierced the skin of his palm. *Take it easy, Jim boy! Remember who depends on you now. Working yourself up into a lather won't change anything for the better.*

And then, without warning, a huge wave of compassion swept over Sanford, compassion for Helen, and sadness at a great love gone wrong. He realized, in cold finality, that an impossible last flicker, a final, dim, wildly irrational hope he had been harbouring, that he and his now dead ex-wife Helen, his beloved Helen, still could have pulled it all together again, had been extinguished savagely. Any chance to retrieve the love of his life had been doomed long since, any pretence to the contrary had been stripped away roughly, and he was now face to face with the cold reality. Helen, his poor, beautiful, suffering Helen, was dead, murdered. That book had been closed and pulped. Sanford could almost hear a number of doors slamming.

*Portals in Literature and Life.* Joe was with him once again.

Sanford thought almost immediately of Helen's parents, Gillian and Philip. At least they would not have to stagger under these dreadful last details about their daughter. This was part of the story that, with luck, they would never know. Lulu was dead. Both the Jeffers brothers were dead. The police would never get to the bottom of it. There might be supposition, theories, but those would never make it beyond the case notes.

The only people who knew now were Sanford and Harold. He cursed the old bastard Harold under his breath. It was Harold who had caused all this. Sanford realized how much he really did hate the old swine. But at the same time he had to admit to a grudging respect for the man's thoroughness and the degree of his awareness.

Images flooded Sanford's head. Helen as a young woman. So engaging, so beautiful, so alive. Flashes of the wild, exhilarating ride that had carried them intimately into each other's lives. Their wedding – small, simple, scintillating. Then the birth of Julia, an event that Sanford had relived hundreds of times.

The image of the past struck him with massive impact. The carriage. The railway carriage that had once contained all his dreams, the place where once he could actively connect past and present, was now decoupled, receding away from him down the line. And it had decoupled everything else as well, was carrying away all that joy, all those unfolding but now frame-frozen dreams, into an irretrievable past.

By a force of will, Sanford thought of the future. The first innocent phrase entering his mind was that it would be what it would be, but that was swept away by a much more forceful and positive statement. *No! It will be what we make it!*

And what would they make it?

Literally, there was a new life to be constructed. Julia had to get to know everything possible about her grandfather, Joe. That meant spending time at Joe's place. But it was at least as important that she get to know her living grandmother, Maria. That meant spending time here in Italy.

A picture was forming in Sanford's mind. And the more he thought about it, even though it seemed slightly crazy, the more comfortable, the more natural, and the more right it felt. Julia would spend time living in Italy. She would get to know her Italian roots. And the shock, the surprisingly pleasant shock for Sanford, was that he would have to do the same, because the roots here, for him, were even closer and deeper.

Sanford knew, without question, what he had to do.

"Gianni? Is something wrong?" They were both standing before him. The concern was evident in Maria's voice.

Sanford wiped his cheeks which were wet from tears.

"There are some painful things I have to get used to Maria, but no, nothing is wrong. In fact, everything is suddenly right."

Sanford led them over to the sofa, and they sat, Julia between him and Maria.

"There's something I have to tell you, Julia..."

# Thirty-one

The beginning of the rest of Sanford's life remained with him as a series of images. The events of the evening of Jeffers' attack faded. An interesting tapestry began to appear as the lives of Maria, Julia, and Sanford began weaving themselves together.

The Italian images were an invitation to discovery.

Julia and Maria spent a week together, and fell naturally into a bond that was between grandmother and granddaughter, but also between friends. Sanford joined them every day at some point, and they had dinner together every evening, at Maria's place, but also at small local restaurants where everyone knew Maria. During the day, Sanford stayed out of their way, mostly, but also found himself a crash course in Italian, and worked at it for several hours each day.

For their third evening meal taken at a local restaurant, they walked ten minutes from Maria's flat to a small osteria, where they were met at the door by a wiry man, tanned deep brown. His dark eyes twinkled. He took Sanford by the hand and said "*Finalmente! Il figlio di Giuseppe! Benvenuto!*", and he kissed Sanford on both cheeks. He hustled them into his small, cosy restaurant, seated them at what turned out to be

Maria's special table, and then began making big hand gestures and issuing instructions to his staff. Bottles of wine appeared on the table, as if dropped there by a genie. Corks popped, and the restaurateur, whose name was Maurizio, appeared to pluck wine glasses from the air and began to fill them. He stopped suddenly.

"*Che vorrebbe bere?*" he said suddenly, standing there waving bottle and glasses in his hands, inclining his head toward Julia. In his head, Sanford translated: *What would she like to drink?* He hoped that Julia would remember the everyday phrases they had been practising, would remember what to say. She demonstrated that she was Joe's granddaughter.

"Vino bianco!"

Maria and Maurizio looked at Julia in surprise. Maurizio did an ecstatic little dance.

"Bravissima! Bravissima! Parla italiano!"

Sanford winked at Julia, gave her a hug, and whispered "Well done!"

Maurizio was in a high-speed chatter with Maria but managed to pour half a glass of white wine for Julia.

"E un po' di acqua minerale", Sanford said.

Maurizio waved his arms energetically, the wine sloshing dangerously near the rim of the glass.

"Formidabile! Tutti e due parlano italiano!"

Somehow, all the glasses were filled, and Maurizio then turned slightly more serious, raised his glass, and said "*Al mio amico Giuseppe!*"

They all drank, to Maurizio's friend Giuseppe, then Maurizio rushed off to welcome someone else.

"Joe and Maurizio knew each other?" Sanford asked Maria.

Maria nodded, chewing a tarallo. "They became quite good friends. Maurizio never got used to the fact that Joe could speak such – what's that word again? – such fluent Italian. Joe came here most days for a drink with Maurizio, and Joe and I ate here probably twice in every week that Joe was in Genoa." Maria looked around the comfortable little restaurant. "I think they miss him."

"We all miss him, Maria."

They went back to Maurizio's place twice more. There were day trips to many spots in and around Genoa, but after Sanford had rearranged their previous travel agenda, they also travelled further afield in Italy. Maria accompanied them to Milan, to Bologna, and of course to Rome. For Sanford, almost every day, but particularly during their days in Rome, there were strong chords of *déjà vu*, and he put that down to many barely remembered fragments that Joe must have related during the time, during the fifteen or so formative years, when Joe had had the strongest influence on the young Sanford. In Rome, they walked themselves almost to death, and Sanford took hundreds of pictures, many of them shots of Julia and Maria in front of well-known sites, but also next to twee restaurants, in small lanes, and in stands of pines. They spent a half day at The Victor Emmanuel Monument, and they took photos of each other at just the spot where Maria and Joe had photographed each other when they were in their twenties.

After a lot of discussion, Maria agreed to travel back with them to Canada for a visit. The remainder of their holiday in Italy was an extended dream, a dream that Sanford was reluctant to see end.

Then there were the arrangements to return to Canada, and Sanford could see that there was a glint of curious expectancy and excitement in Maria's eyes.

During the flight back to Toronto, Sanford was lost in thought.

Despite buying a seat for Maria almost at the last minute, he did manage to bargain a swap so that the three of them could sit together. Maria wanted the aisle seat, and Julia wouldn't sit anywhere except next to Maria, so Sanford was shunted to the window. He watched the two of them as they read comics in Italian, but soon Julia began nodding off. Maria glanced across at Sanford occasionally, but her expression was impossible to read. Expectant, certainly. But there was something else as well. Something connected to Joe.

Without having to think about it, plans began forming in Sanford's mind. What they would do in Canada. Return trips to Italy. But he could also see important discussions that would unfold.

There was Aileen.

Aileen had been spared, by Joe, from what might have been a lonely and sadly barren life. Joe, who must have become early on a friend and confidant, had sensed a mutual advantage, and had entrusted Jim to her to raise as a son of her own. And she had done a job that was second to none, but the price she paid was a perpetual fear of having her dream shattered. That was why Joe had agreed reluctantly not to tell Sanford about his origins. Aileen was petrified that *her* son Jim would become distant, or, worse, that she would lose him altogether. Sanford's gratitude to Aileen was now fathomless.

There was Joe.

By agreeing to keep Aileen's secret, Joe had also committed himself to silence on being Sanford's father. So he had raised a son without the son ever knowing that his friend and mentor was really his father, at least not while the father was alive. It was clear to Sanford that Joe had not intended this to be an arrangement permanent for all time, that Sanford would have learned the full story of his own past following Aileen's sudden death, if fate then hadn't taken Joe as well. But even given all that, Joe could not leave a written record of Sanford's past, which Sanford would then undoubtedly read, in case Joe happened to die before Aileen, thereby leaving her to answer all the tough questions, and placing her squarely before the greatest fear in her life: the risk of alienation from her son Jim. Even for someone having Joe's strength, what a sacrifice this must have been! Joe had also kept from Maria the fact that she had a granddaughter. Why? Having had time to think the matter through, this now seemed pretty evident to Sanford. What could Maria have done knowing that fact? Well, nothing, without the potential of causing both Aileen and Joe great grief, if somehow the truth had slipped to Sanford, especially while Aileen was still alive. And if she had known and simply kept quiet? To put Maria in the position of having to live with that bottled-up knowledge would have been cruel on Joe's part. So, Joe had just kept quiet. Even Aileen's death Joe had kept from Maria, at least until Joe had had a chance to unveil the full picture for Sanford, an outcome cruelly short-circuited by Joe's sudden death. Chance and circumstance had rendered it a no-win situation for everyone.

Sanford now was reconciled also to the dark element in his past.

Harold.

Sanford was convinced now that Harold was almost amoral. Almost. He probably did have, at one time, some considerable feeling for Aileen, but he had no guiding light on how to act in concert with those feelings, and with respect to Aileen he had behaved abominably. At best, he was a man ill-equipped to handle even the simplest moral situations. At worst, he was somebody whose serious psychological defects left the deck stacked against him. At bottom, he was an inveterate criminal and liar, and his refined and accomplished low cunning had turned these characteristics practically into an art form. It was Harold's actions that had caused their paths to cross those of the unspeakable Jeffers brothers. In the end, Harold had taken the easy way out and just bought himself off from any perceived commitments. He was now out of their lives, and good riddance.

In Canada, Sanford treated Maria to all the touristy things. He recalled images of Maria in his condo in Toronto, and like all first-time visitors, she stared for half an hour at a lake so big that one couldn't see the other side. They strolled through the university.

"Here it is, Maria", Sanford said, pointing to a large ornate building.

"This is where Joe attended university?"

Sanford nodded. "Yes. Right here."

"Can we go in?" she asked.

"Certainly."

They wandered the halls for about fifteen minutes. Maria peered into rooms, while Sanford scanned the walls until he found what he wanted.

"Look at this, Maria."

Maria gazed at the class photo, and it took her only a couple of minutes to find him.

"It's Joe!" she exclaimed loudly, then looked around guiltily.

Turning back to the photograph, she gazed at it for several minutes. A large smile spread across her face, then tears were coursing down her cheeks.

"He was such a wonderful, handsome young man!"

They stood in front of the picture a bit longer, then wandered out of the building. Maria wanted to know where Sanford had studied, and he showed her the buildings where his classes had been. They strolled back across King's College Circle to Hart House, Sanford bought them a cup of coffee each, and they sat at one of the small outdoor tables, sipping.

The following day, Sanford said to Maria "Today we're going for a plane ride". There were questions and objections, but Sanford just herded Maria along, and she smiled at the fabricated mystery. At the airport on the Toronto Islands, Sanford had chartered a small plane and pilot for a day. They took off and they flew over the city, to a steady monologue from Sanford. They flew over Stanley Falls, over the lakes and forests in central Ontario, over part of Georgian Bay, over Niagara Falls, and back to Toronto along the shore of Lake Ontario. It was a day that left Maria dumbfounded.

And they spent two weeks at Joe's place.

This was the hardest for Maria. Joe's essence was everywhere, and she spent an hour just walking through the house, touching everything. She had known Joe only in Italy, and seeing the context for his life in Canada delivered to her the combined shock and delight of learning a whole new side of someone she had known intimately.

"Let me give you a proper tour, Maria", and she smiled and nodded eagerly.

The kitchen and the library were the first stops.

"This place was a second home to me", Sanford said, running his hand over a shelf in the library.

"Joe said that you sat here and read", Maria said, pointing to the large wing chair.

"I did. But Joe also educated me here. I think I learned more in this room than in all the school rooms I have ever sat in."

Maria wandered along, looking at the books. The love, the wistfulness, the gratitude at seeing something that she had probably seen only in photographs, were clearly written on her face.

They drifted outside. Joe's garden dominated the area behind the house, and in its order and completeness it spoke eloquently of Joe.

Maria turned when she heard the "woof" that had become so familiar to Sanford.

"And this", he said, "is Reggie".

Maria moved toward the dog, his tail wagged, hesitantly at first, then in welcome.

"Reggie", she said, and knelt down to greet the dog.

Reggie was now in full welcome, and he began licking Maria's face while she wept and hugged him, knowing how Joe had loved all his Reggie dogs.

They walked through the barn, and Maria ran her hands over the wood-burnt names of the cows.

"This is where you and Joe milked the cows?"

Sanford nodded, but wanted to get away from the barn as soon as he could, away from the thing that was trying to hook into his brain again.

Over the next few days, they weeded Joe's vegetable garden, Maria picked flowers from Joe's flower gardens and arranged them in attractive bunches in the kitchen, and the three of them prepared meals together.

Most memorably, they spent time in *The Recipe Cops.* In Respighi's Copse. On her first visit, Maria just sat on one of the large bench stones and took in the place. The pine needles underfoot were soft, springy, and provided natural acoustic damping. The pines sighed, above and around them. The great pieces of limestone were smooth and cool. She hummed snatches of tunes from *The Pines of Rome*. And all around was quiet, seclusion, sanctity.

"Joe told me so much about this place, so many times, how you and he loved to spend time here…", and her voice faded as she gazed around at the large pines and up into their branches, listening to their whispered secrets.

"But now that I'm here ... I can hardly believe it. It's beautiful!"

She ran her hand over the large cool table stone.

"He told me about having these stones made, and how they were put together, and how you both poured cups of water over them..."

"The Recipe Cops", she murmured, after a long pause, almost in meditation.

There was another long pause.

"Joe is here", she said quietly. "This is the place to say goodbye to him."

And then they talked about the new life, unexpected until just a few weeks ago, that now stretched before the three of them who remained.

# Acknowledgements

My thanks to Walter Cimaschi, whose advice and suggestions make it look as though I know more Italian than, in fact, I do.

My thanks to my wife, Maggie, my strongest and most sympathetic critic.

CPSIA information can be obtained at www.ICGtesting.com
Printed in the USA
LVOW07s2358160916

505007LV00002B/5/P

9 781771 80185